Regal - Text copyright © 1
Cover Art by Emmy Ellis @ stu... .... © 2025

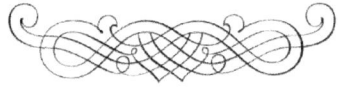

All Rights Reserved

Regal is a work of fiction. All characters, places, and events are from the author's imagination. Any resemblance to persons, living or dead, events or places is purely coincidental.

The author respectfully recognises the use of any and all trademarks.

With the exception of quotes used in reviews, this book may not be reproduced or used in whole or in part by any means existing without written permission from the author.

Warning: The unauthorised reproduction or distribution of this copyrighted work is illegal. No part of this book may be scanned, uploaded, or distributed via the Internet or any other means, electronic or print, without the author's written permission. The author does not give permission for any part of this book to be used in AI.

Published by Five Pyramids Press, Suite 1a 34 West Street,
Retford, England, DN22 6ES
ISBN: 9798315500957

REGAL

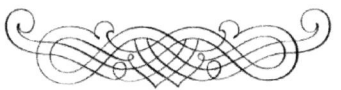

Emmy Ellis

Chapter One

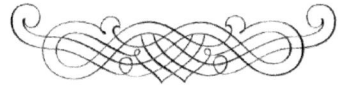

Fantasy sat in a back room in the parlour at The Angel, her heart tickering fast, the squeezing dread of impending doom wreaking havoc with her stomach. She needed the loo really badly but didn't want to use a public toilet. She'd always been funny about that. Having to share a bathroom in that bloody house… She'd had to get used to it, but she'd hated it all the same. Thank God she didn't have to do that anymore.

She had to keep reminding herself she was safe, no one could hurt her—well, they could, but she'd come here to ask the twins to hide her until she could return to her normal life. What if she wasn't believed? What if The Brothers told her to fuck off home? She looked like a right scabby tart in these clothes, especially the coat, so it wouldn't be a surprise if they turfed her out. Her hair, a greasy-at-the-roots mess, didn't exactly do her any favours either.

She didn't resemble Bluebell, the woman they knew. Would that go in her favour? Add authenticity to what she had to tell them? And would they think she was weird when she said she wanted to be called Fantasy now, considering she'd thought of that name under duress when she'd been barked at to come up with one for her new role? She doubted they'd understand that as Fantasy, she'd oddly been stronger, had more confidence, when really, she should have been at her lowest ebb.

She hadn't expected to be back here, *ever*. She'd been kept in that house with the boarded-up windows with no chance of escape. The amount of times she'd thought she'd die there, shot in the head then chucked outside while her captors, Mocha and Julian, dug her grave. She hadn't been there that long, but it had felt like forever.

She should never have tried to get one last customer that night outside the Noodle. That customer had been Mocha, the bastard who bowed down to the High Priest and got women to do whatever he said—and he bossed Julian around, too, the bloke who looked after the ladies trapped in the house. She doubted many people would believe her if she said Julian was a nice man, that he didn't seem to belong in that environment, but it was true. For the whole time she'd known him, he'd always said he didn't want to hurt any of them, almost pleaded with them to do as they were told at times so he didn't have to resort to violence, while in other instances he made out he was scary and shouted at them. It was obvious he was only passing on what Mocha had told him to say anyway, and those orders would have trickled down from the High Priest.

The hierarchy had been made clear to her right from the start: the men had differing levels of power, the women were underlings with none.

Except that was bullshit—Fantasy had taken her power back and escaped.

The night Mocha had taken her would live in her memory forever. Anyone who'd been abducted wasn't likely to forget it due to the harrowing nature of it all—well, harrowing once she'd realised she hadn't picked up a customer and it was unlikely she'd ever go home. She hoped to maybe bury it in the back of her mind one day, but it was too raw at the minute.

She only felt a little bit bad after running from Jerry's house last night, the place the women had been taken to. She'd left three other women behind with Julian, but one of them was an undercover police officer; Empress now had the responsibility of freeing everybody, something Fantasy had vowed to do before the copper had come along, and she hoped that included Julian who was as much a prisoner as they were.

But last night she'd had to think of herself; her sole instinct was to get away to freedom, even though Julian, Mocha, and the High Priest knew her address—or so they'd told her. She supposed that was their way of threatening her, letting her know if she managed to escape them they'd go to her place and collect her again. She didn't trust them as far as she could throw them, so she wasn't about to risk going home. Julian would have passed it on to Mocha that she'd escaped by now—he hadn't been able to follow her or force her to go with him and the others when Empress had spotted the flash of blue lights from the bathroom window, because they'd all had to leg it quickly.

It just so happened Fantasy had gone out the front while they'd gone out the back. As she'd been running down the street, the euphoria of liberty dashing through her veins, a car had stopped. A man had got out, a detective holding up ID, and at the time she'd worried it was another trick, he was someone sent by Mocha or the High Priest to whisk her away to the boarded-up house. But DI Taylor had insisted he was a copper and that she should go to the police station. Something about him had put her at ease, more so when a patrol car turned up and an officer opened the window and spoke to him, calling him sir. She'd trusted her instincts and gone to the station, and that meant she hadn't been able to get to the parlour until this morning, Sunday.

Now, after no sleep, she waited for the twins. A young woman had shown her into this room, someone Fantasy hadn't known when she'd worked for Debbie, saying the usual two ladies who manned the front desk were both off poorly with the sniffles and she'd stepped in to help. Carly, her real name was, but at work she called herself Blossom.

Carly had made a pot of tea and brought in a bacon sandwich made by the pub chef. The meal had gone quite a way to fortifying Fantasy's flagging brain and body, but all she really wanted was a bath and a proper good sleep. Except she had an interview with George and Greg to get through first, not only because they'd probably find out who the High Priest and Mocha were before the police did, even with Empress working undercover, but she needed somewhere to live until the men were discovered. As far as she was concerned, her flat was a massive no-go area.

A knock at the door had her jumping, and she stared at it, waiting for it to open. When no one came in, she said, "Yes?"

"It's Carly. Do you want some more tea?"

"No, thanks. You can come in, you know."

Carly popped her head in. "The twins will be here in ten minutes."

Fantasy's stomach rolled over. "Okay, thanks for letting me know."

Carly retreated and closed the door.

Fantasy rested her head back on the sofa and closed her eyes, the pull of sleep threatening to drag her under. She forced herself to lean forward and stare at the floor, her eyes stinging from where she was so tired. The ten minutes dragged, and when another knock on the door startled the shit out of her, even though she'd been expecting it, she got to her feet, conscious she had flimsy lingerie and high heels on from being at Jerry's, plus an old woollen black coat someone at the police station had given her out of lost property. It smelled funny, mould mixed with sour milk, but it had been so cold when she'd left the station that she was grateful for it.

The door opened once again. George entered first, giving her a nod and sitting on the sofa opposite, Greg following him and closing the door. Fantasy sat and thought about how she could make them believe this completely bizarre story. Maybe *because* it was bizarre, they'd know she told the truth.

"So, what can we help you with?" George asked. "Carly said it was *very* important and couldn't wait. I hope for your sake that's true because we don't like getting out of bed earlier than usual on a Sunday unless we absolutely have to."

So he was letting her know he was already narked, which didn't bode well. Still, she had something to tell them whether they wanted to hear it or not, and considering it had all happened on their Estate, then they could fucking well deal with it.

"You know those women who've been on the news for months, the ones taken from the industrial estate?" She may as well start from before she'd been dragged into this mess. Besides, it had caught their attention, most likely because news of those women had been on the telly and social media before she'd been abducted herself.

"Go on," George said.

"I know where they were taken—not the address because I've never known that, just that it's a house and I lived in it. Anyway, I was also taken, but it was from outside your pub."

"Which one?" Greg asked.

"The Noodle. I was touting for business because there's no cameras." She held up a hand to stop either of them from shouting at her. "And before you say anything, believe me, I wish to God I hadn't gone there."

"So you're saying the person who took those three women also took you."

"Yes."

"And are they okay?"

"I've been told they're dead. They were killed before I got taken—that's the reason I *was* taken because I had to fill one of their places. Two more were nabbed the same night as me, one round the side of The Angel actually, and the other near Kitchen Street, then more recently someone else came to join us. She's a copper, put herself out there deliberately in the hope she'd get abducted. She got picked up at the industrial estate."

"Who are the other two?"

"I don't know their real names, but they go by Pearl and Candy. The High Priest expects us to make new names up when we start working for him."

George's eyes widened. "Err, say that again? The high fucking what? What the shitting hell's *that*? Were you taken into a cult or something?"

"The stuff that went on of a Saturday night was a bit like a cult, I suppose. I'll tell you about the rituals in a minute—"

"Rituals? Jesus pissing wept!"

"—but being in the house was actually okay, believe it or not, because we lived with Julian."

"Who's he?"

"The man I gather was told to look after us."

"That's a weird way of putting it. What do you mean, told?"

"I don't think he wants to do it."

"Did he tell you that?"

"No, it's just a feeling I got from him. Anyway, I was taken from outside the Noodle and thought it was a normal pickup, but this bloke wasn't my average customer because he said he wanted to talk rather than have sex."

"Do many punters only want that?"

"They're few and far between, but it's not unusual enough for me not to have gone with him or to have queried it. Anyway, he said he'd prefer to drive around rather than go and park up somewhere. The only thing he wanted me to do was to wear a blindfold."

"That's a red flag straight away," Greg muttered.

Fantasy let out a wry laugh. "You'd think it *wouldn't* be, considering what I do for a living, but yes, it did set alarm bells off, but I was already in the car and he'd handed over a hundred quid, which was more than I'd have got for having sex so… He *did* chat, though. Talked about a woman who could have been his wife but his choices in life had meant she was the 'one who'd got away', and it seemed like a genuine conversation, you know? Like he needed someone to listen. I still think he was telling me the truth there, even though later on he said it was all bollocks."

"What happened then?"

"We drove quite a way, I'd say for fifteen minutes. Obviously, I'd put the blindfold on so couldn't see, but I don't think it was a straight run from the Noodle to the house."

"What gave you that idea?"

"Because since then, I know how he abducts people because he took me with him the last time when he picked up the copper. Going by the conversation between Mocha and Julian in the front, he drove around a housing estate for a while. So basically, what I'm saying is, I couldn't work out where the boarded-up house is."

"Hang on. You were picked up by Mocha on his own, so how come you and Julian went the last time to nab someone else?"

"Because of Tara."

"Who's that?"

"She threw herself out of Mocha's car one time. They told us she was dead from the injuries, but Empress said she's alive." Fantasy went on to fill them in on that side of the story.

"Blimey. You said about rituals," George prompted. "Tell me about those."

She explained what happened within a stone circle that was set up at various locations, places she couldn't name because she'd always been blindfolded on the journeys. The stones themselves were fake, hollow, and taken to a different site on Saturday nights. Recalling what had happened after that was as chilling and surreal as it had been when she'd told DI Taylor and his colleague, DC Misty something or other.

"Fucking hell," George said when she'd finished. "When I get my hands on those bastards…"

"But that's the thing, unless the undercover copper there manages to find out who the hell Mocha and the High Priest really are, and she can even escape the house or wherever, who's to say they'll ever be arrested?"

George scratched the side of his head. "What else went on?"

Fantasy told them the rest and how she'd come to get away, her aim as she'd left Jerry's house to get to The Angel as quickly as possible so Lisa, the manager, could contact the twins. Only, she'd been waylaid by the detective.

"So you were supposed to have sex with this Jerry fella, but the police came, blue lights flashing, the lot?"

"Yes."

"This could prove more challenging because the pigs are involved," Greg said. "We could be going to the same places they are during our investigation, and I don't really want them to know we're on the case as well."

"There's always disguises," George said. "And we could use the taxi or the van. So this Jerry…seeing as you got away, you must know what street he lives in."

She nodded. "Number four Alding Close."

George raised his eyebrows and stared at his brother. "We'll go and see our snitch."

Greg nodded. "I'm surprised she never got hold of us, considering the police were in that street last night."

"Maybe she thought we'd have heard about it so didn't bother." George smiled at Fantasy. "How do you fancy renting a flat from us? We've got a few."

"I was going to say that I need somewhere else to go, but it only has to be for a while until you've found Mocha and the High Priest. I like the flat I've already got, so I just want somewhere to hunker down for a bit until you tell me it's okay to go home."

"Like a safe house?"

"I'd like to disappear so I can get my head around what's happened to me. I told you the amount of people who came to the rituals. I couldn't see any of their faces because they wore masks, but they could see mine, and with no clue who they are, I wouldn't know them from Adam if they saw me on the street and let Mocha know they've seen me."

"Are you all right staying at a safe house on your own or would you prefer us to put one of our men in there with you?"

"Is it alarmed and whatnot?"

"Of course it fucking is."

"Then I don't see why I shouldn't stay there by myself." She gestured to her outfit. "I'll need some clothes, though, and this coat can go straight in the bloody bin. It was given to me down the cop shop, so fuck knows who owned it before me."

Greg stood. "I'll nip to Tesco to get you some gear. If you don't mind me asking, what size are you?"

"Fourteen in clothes and six in shoes. Sports bras will do, ta."

Greg left the room.

"There's toiletries and everything at all of our safe houses," George said. "I'll let our man, Will, know to go and top up the fridge. The freezer and cupboards will already be full—they're restocked after every visitor has left."

Relieved she'd be out of the picture for the foreseeable, she had to ask, "How much rent and whatever will I owe you for going to the safe house? It's just I've got a couple of grand in the bank to cover the bills for my flat for a while—they're all on direct debit, everything was paid out of my savings while I've been gone, but seeing as I won't be able to work…"

"Don't worry about it. Greg won't be long with your clothes, then we can get you to the safe house, and after that, we'll be on a mission to find out which bastards did this to you. Just out of interest, do you know the undercover copper's real name?"

"I actually don't remember if she even told me."

"Not to worry. We'll put the feelers out, and someone will come up trumps with who she is."

Fantasy rested her head back and closed her eyes. "Thank you for helping me. God, I'm so fucking tired."

"Have a little sleep. I'll leave you to it for a bit."

Chapter Two

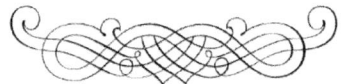

Detective Sergeant Vee Little sat at her desk in the Serious Crime Squad incident room. People coughed, cleared their throats, or muttered amongst themselves, the air full of too many different aftershaves and deodorant scents. Cloying, what with the heating on full blast—it was like a bloody sauna. She didn't want to join one of the many discussions *going on around her while the team waited for DI Richard Taylor to start the meeting. She'd rather stay in her own head than push herself onto her colleagues — they likely wouldn't want her in their lives outside of work anyway.*

Stop being negative.

Life had been a bag of shite lately. She had no partner at home, no kids, no parents to visit, seeing as she'd cut herself off from them years ago. Their obsession with each other and booze meant no room for her. Work was the most interesting thing she had going on, but even then it had turned stale recently. Or maybe that was her. Maybe, no matter how hard she was trying, she couldn't pull herself out of the depressive rut she'd fallen into when her last relationship had gone down the pan. When Ross had left, tired of her always working (even though she'd warned him from the start that's what coppers did), she'd spiralled, allowing the grief of their parting to drag her right down.

It had been calming at first, to wallow, to stay in bed and hide under the covers, to cry without seeing anyone for days on end. She'd called in sick, making out she had the flu, and had existed on whatever was in her kitchen cupboards and the freezer, in the end going without milk in her tea just so she didn't have to get dressed and go to the shop or answer the door to a delivery driver. Having a shower was a massive big deal—she'd talked herself out of it more often than not, until she couldn't stand her own smell.

That first shower after a hibernation period of terrible mourning had been the first step to poking her head out of the cave and sniffing the air to find that spring lurked just around the corner. God, had that really been a year ago, and she was still suffering? Well then, she'd likely cared about Ross more than any of the others. She must have done if she'd allowed him to move in with her, if she'd allowed herself to believe in a happy ever after. And two years wasn't anything to sniff at, was it? It was a long time to be with someone. All right, she hadn't racked up the decades like some of her old friends (the ones she'd abandoned) who were still loved-up and happy with their soul mates, but she had to remind herself that having someone in your life or in your bed didn't define you. Happy still existed for single people.

For the past twelve months, she'd tried to pull up her bootstraps, get herself out of the fog of despair and into a better way of thinking. Being more upbeat. Opting for a positive response rather than a negative, which meant she had to really think before she spoke. It was hard work, training herself to be Miss Smiley when all she wanted was to scream and rant and rave. Give a few people what for.

She snapped out of her head at a clap from the front of the room.

Taylor came to stand beside the interactive board. His blond hair, peppered with grey at the temples, was a bit of a mullet, and he regularly got ribbed about it. No amount of light-hearted bullying would make him cut it, though. "Okay, so I've been in a meeting with DCI Black, and we're going to make a move on Operation Shuttle, the abductions we've been working on. As none of the three women have been discovered yet, and it's frustrating as fuck for us all when no leads have come to anything, we're going to go with Vee's suggestion of using an officer as bait."

She sat up straighter, her frown deep, because surely he hadn't just admitted he agreed with her. And did that mean he was using her *as bait or that he was going with the suggestion that* someone *should be? She'd been undercover before, but only for small jobs. Still, she was more than capable, and she'd proved that already.*

She glanced over at Misty who was more likely to want the job, but she didn't look anything like the women who'd been taken so far. She wasn't brunette or skinny enough, and Vee was.

Taylor was saying something else, but she hadn't caught it.

"Sorry, sir, what did you say?"

"What the bloody hell have you reverted to calling me 'sir' for?"

"Sorry again," she said.

"What I asked you was whether you were up for it. Waiting in the abduction spot for however many nights it takes for someone to pick you up, if they even do."

She knew why he'd added that last part. Ever since the third woman had gone missing, which had elevated the abductions to a higher level on the news, more airtime granted, no sex workers had been on that street. For once, they'd listened and stayed away, but it had taken three snatches for them to fully understand how serious this was. The abductors might not bother to return there, they'd kept away for months now, but it was the only solid lead the team had, other than a dark car being used.

"Um, yes, I can do that," Vee said. "But there's the stone rituals I'm working on…"

Tara Eccles had been abducted from a different street corner. She'd managed to get away in the end, but prior to that she'd been blindfolded and taken to a house with the windows boarded up with shutters from the inside—they'd been screwed tight. Three other women had been there, along with a man calling himself Julian who looked after them and ferried them from the house to the location of the stones. They were a little like Stonehenge, standing in a circle, but others were more like beds in the middle, which the women were instructed to stretch themselves out on and—

Vee didn't want to think about what had then played out. It had been uncomfortable and shocking when Tara had explained what had gone on. Since the blindfold had been in play during the journey, and it had been dark when they'd arrived at the location, Tara had no idea where the stones were. All she'd picked up on were tiny spots of light in the background, which may have been a town or a city, and that they were in a massive field. The stones themselves, she swore blind they felt fake, like off a film set. That made sense, because no real stone monuments had been found in the area. Tara couldn't determine the length of time it had taken to get from the house to the stone setup.

Vee was the only one left working the case as it had gone cold, but she'd always wondered whether it was linked to the abductions in Operation Shuttle.

Taylor glanced at Misty. "You'll be all right to take over Operation Ritual in Vee's absence, won't you?"

Misty nodded, but she didn't look too chuffed to have been handed that job—it was tedious, going over and over the same files, trying to find a clue. If Vee wasn't mistaken, Misty would have preferred to be an abductee.

"Right then," Taylor said, "we'll go through what needs to happen, then we'll set things up for tomorrow night. I want us to go over and over this throughout the afternoon so we're all on exactly the same page. There's no room for fucking up here, and if Vee's hunch has been right all along and Shuttle is linked to Ritual, then we just might be able to kill two birds with one stone."

Taylor was a bloody decent DI, but in her opinion, he didn't give the team enough praise, nor did he agree with some of the things they said, even though it was glaringly obvious that what they'd said was right. He was the sort to need a couple of days to let things percolate, but in a job like theirs, there wasn't always the luxury of that amount of time. Still, he always got the job done, but she worried that if she went undercover and he didn't act quickly enough at certain times, she may be in danger.

"Go and get a coffee and a sandwich," he said, "and we'll reconvene here in half an hour. This is going to be a very delicate and risky operation, so I need

everyone's heads in the game. Food will help with that."

Vee got up and left the room before he could keep her back for one of his 'chats' that he swore would only take two minutes but ended up being more than ten. She didn't want to miss out on a full lunch break so shot down the corridor to get to the canteen before a queue formed. She arrived with only two people ahead of her, and when her turn came, she ordered a toasted cheese and ham sandwich, a cinnamon bun, and a latte.

She took her food on a tray and chose a table in the far corner, sitting and facing the wall to make it clear she didn't want anyone joining her. She needed to just 'be' for a few minutes, to breathe. Aware that this behaviour kept people away when she was supposed to be following her therapist's advice in drawing people closer, she cursed herself for falling on bad habits. She was meant to be taking up offers of going out for a drink or a meal. She was meant to be accepting invitations to go to someone's house for a night of board games. She was supposed to be putting herself out there, but something wasn't right since Ross had left her, and she couldn't seem to find the oomph for anything.

Maybe this undercover job would give her the kick up the arse she needed.

The afternoon meeting had been boring, and when they'd gone over the operation for the eighth time, Vee had wanted to scream. Finally free, she walked out of the station with her mission firmly cemented in her mind, so that was something. They'd imagined several scenarios where things could go wrong, but she'd be followed after the abduction by members of the team, so she wasn't too worried.

In the darkness and slight chill of the March evening, having done two hours of overtime because the bloody meeting had run over, she scanned the car park, as she always did, for anyone who shouldn't be there. It pissed her off that as a woman she had to do this. Everything was clear, so she sat in her car, locked herself in, and got on the road.

The drive home was stop-and-start bullshit and full of frustration. She beeped her horn at two different people and stuck her middle finger up at another, all of them deserving it because they'd pulled out in front of her when it was her right of way. Her irritation level reached its peak when there was a set of lights up ahead due to roadworks, but she nipped down a side street and went home that way instead. She parked and all but launched herself up the steps to the Victorian house that had been converted into three flats. She lived right at the top and not for the first time cursed the amount of stairs she had to take.

She opened her front door and went inside, locking up. Two quick kicks sent her shoes flying in different directions, who cared where they landed. She put her boot slippers on and went straight into the kitchen to pour a glass of wine. The one thing she'd continued to do after Ross had left was make dinner for herself, even if it was only cheap noodles with tomato ketchup on top. Today she had a HelloFresh meal, so she got on with cooking that while sipping her drink, topping up every time it reached the halfway point.

What she should have done since Ross left was stop it with the wine. They'd only ever had one glass each per night, but these days, some evenings she progressed to three or four. Many times she'd laughed at herself for becoming a cliché book detective, full of angst and alcohol, wading her way through the criminal fraternity to give her life some kind of fucking, shitty meaning.

"Piss off," she muttered and dished her food up.

She ate and went through the case notes of Operations Shuttle and Ritual. Every time she compared notes, it was glaringly obvious to her the cases were linked, and now that Taylor agreed with her, Vee didn't feel so bad that some of the team had ridiculed her, saying she had too much of a vivid imagination and should rein it in. At one point she'd believed them, her depression only listening to the bad things they said about her rather than the good. If she could be arsed, she'd feel smug that she was right and they were wrong, but she didn't even have it in her to do that.

Things had to change.

Once her food was gone, she went through the notes she'd made during the meeting.

1: NEED CLOTHING TO PASS AS A SEX WORKER.

2: COMFORTABLE SHOES IN CASE I HAVE TO RUN.

3: PICK A WORKING NAME.

4: ALWAYS BE AWARE THE TEAM HAVE MY BACK.

That last one was all very well, but police operations did go wrong, and she'd be a fool to think this one would go without a hitch. There was the blindfold aspect for a start. She'd probably be bundled into the back of the vehicle. While she agreed with the specially adapted knickers with the pouch in them, where she'd place a burner phone, if she was patted down by her abductor then that phone would be found and taken away.

She'd have no contact with Taylor and the team.

Basically, she could well be fucked.

Chapter Three

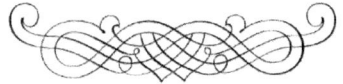

Number four Alding Close was dead opposite Sandra Deptford's house—one of the twins' snitches. She'd come to be in their employ during the last big incident that they'd had to deal with. She lived in one of the most avoid-if-you-can streets on the Cardigan Estate— not only were some of the people the kind who gave humanity a bad name, but the council really ought to think about pulling their finger out and doing up the facades. George would bet a penny to a pound the interiors needed sorting out, too.

"Look at the fucking state of this area," he whispered. "It's got worse since we were here last."

The old wooden windows needed replacing—there was no point keep painting over the rot—and the pebbledash outer walls could do with a good clean, green mould displayed in places. It appeared many residents had bought their own front doors, because as was usual with council or housing association homes, they normally all matched and these didn't. The old that remained were wrecked by the weather and were a security risk—one kick, and a burglar would be in. It shouldn't have to be that way, people begging the council to fix what was broken, but many requests landed on deaf ears. George saw enough of it on social media to know that the situation between tenants and landlords was precarious at best.

Jerry's door was of the new variety. Previous to them approaching it, George and Greg had scoped out the street to catch any sign that police officers were still hanging around. They'd also got hold of Colin, their copper, to ask him to get any information he could regarding the situation here last night. Apparently, Jerry hadn't said an awful lot in his interview other than he'd paid for women to give him a good time but they'd left without fulfilling their agreement. As for this High Priest, Mocha, and Julian, Jerry had made out he didn't know who they were. Utter crap, to be honest, when Bluebell/Fantasy had told them Julian had been in the house with them.

As for the undercover copper, she was called Vee Little.

George lifted a hand to knock on the door. His patience only ran to him waiting for about thirty seconds, then he knocked again. It seemed to take ages before anybody came, but soon enough they were presented with a man of indeterminate age. He could be anything from fifty to eighty, gingery-grey hair in a mullet, the top swept back with gel, the ends cotton-wool thick. He glanced past Greg's right shoulder at their taxi parked at the kerb, then back at the twins, his frown deep.

"Good morning," George said.

"Err, what do you want?"

"We want you to tell us what happened last night."

Jerry looked them up and down, taking in their beards and wigs and glasses, their tracksuit bottoms and ugly fleece jackets. "What are you, journalists?"

George leaned close. "We're The Brothers, and I suggest you let us in."

Jerry paled. "This is all I fucking need."

He turned and walked down the hallway, so George lost no time in following him. He left Greg to close the door and found Jerry in the kitchen. He stood at the sink filling a kettle. No sign of a coffeemaker, so George would be a good boy and accept an instant should he be offered one. If he wasn't, he'd make it clear he should have been.

He took the liberty of sitting at a scutty wooden table on one of two chairs which didn't match and appeared to have come from one of the many front gardens down here that boasted a crap-ton of rubbish. George resolved to sort out the state of this street himself, but that was something to be done after their chat with Jerry.

Greg walked into the kitchen and took the other chair, which George was pleased about. It meant Jerry would be left standing. He'd be more exposed, unable to hide shaking hands or a tapping foot under the table. The man still had his back to them, so George raised his eyebrows at his brother to get his take on things. Greg shrugged, which was no fucking help at all.

Tosser.

With the kettle rumbling and Jerry having placed three cups on the worktop, he turned and scrutinised George and Greg. He must have accepted they were the twins as he nodded to himself in confirmation. Maybe he'd seen them somewhere before and recognised their eyes, the only bit about them that would give them away. They hadn't bothered with contacts today.

"I can understand why you'd come here after what happened last night, but I'm telling you, I only paid for four girls to come and entertain me and I didn't get what I handed over my hard-earned cash for. One of them legged it out the front, and the other three fucked off out the back with J…with the man they live with."

"It sounded to me like you were going to say his name," George said, "only you remembered you probably weren't supposed to, but I caught it, that little slip of the tongue, and I'll ask you nicely if you'll tell me what that name is that begins with J."

"I can't. I told the police last night that I've got no idea who he is, because if the pigs get wind of the organisation who supplies the girls then that's it, my life's over. The same applies to me telling you two."

"But the police can't force you to tell them. We can."

"Please, I don't want to die."

"But you will either way if you don't tell us what we want to know. If you tell us and the organisation finds out, they'll kill you. If you don't tell us, then we'll kill you, it really is that simple."

"Then I don't win."

"Of course you do. You spill the beans to us, but we'll inform people that you wouldn't open your mouth. Word will get about that you're trustworthy, you can keep a secret, and the organisation will leave you alone."

"But they won't, because you'll go after J, and it's going to be obvious it was me who opened my mouth. I'm not stupid."

"I think, after we've had that cup of coffee you're going to make us, that we ought to take you off to keep you safe until all this has blown over. From what we've been told, these people might well be a bit too dangerous to allow you to stay at home." George had no intention of keeping the man safe, unless you counted stringing him up in the cellar of the warehouse and forcing him to give up information.

Jerry nodded. "That's the best bet. One of them has already been on the phone to me, saying I don't have to pay for the next visit because I didn't get what I paid for last night. I told them we're better off not doing it here again. For all I know, the police could be watching the gaff."

"So what exactly did you pay for?"

"Sex."

"And that's in place of the rituals. Right."

Jerry seemed surprised George knew about them, his eyebrows shooting up, then he turned, maybe to hide his expression, and got on with pouring boiled water into the cups, adding coffee. He went to the fridge to take the milk out and put that on the table along with two cups and some sugar. It seemed a long time for none of them to be speaking, George and Greg waiting for him to give some kind of response regarding the rituals, but it looked like the bloke was stalling for time;

he took a tin out of the cupboard, removed the lid, and placed biscuits on the table.

No custard creams or bourbons. What a whopping black mark against him. The next best thing were chocolate Hobnobs. George took one and munched on it, pouring milk into his coffee, adding sugar, content enough to sit there in silence until Jerry couldn't stand it any longer and filled it with gibberish, as most guilty people did. But Jerry helped himself to a biscuit, too, and George cursed himself because his patience took a battering; he was going to be the one to cave in first.

"Are you a red disciple or a watcher?" George asked.

"I've been both. I prefer being a disciple, though."

"I bet you do. Much more involved." While George didn't have anything against the rituals and that kind of thing if it was done with everyone's consent, he did have a problem when women were kidnapped for the sole purpose of being laid out on stones and having men perform sexual acts on them against their will.

"I get it that some people don't understand it," Jerry said, "but we're not doing any harm, and we're paying them for the privilege."

"Except you're not. None of them receive a penny. All they get is food and lodgings."

Jerry frowned. "I didn't know that."

"And if you did? Would it have made a difference?"

Jerry's cheeks turned pink, as did the tips of his ears. "Probably not, no."

Another reason George would be taking him to the warehouse.

He took another Hobnob from the tin, checking on Greg from the corner of his eye. He looked disgusted and about to flip his lid.

"Yeah, I really think we ought to keep you safe, Jerry," Greg said. "Even better, we'll hole you up in one of our nice little places—a cottage in the forest, in fact, where you can hang out to your heart's content. We can go and pay J a visit and make sure he gets the message that you're not to be messed with, else he'll have us to deal with. We can even kill him for you if you like."

Jerry stared at the biscuit tin as though hoping it contained all the answers he needed. "But I don't know where he lives. I don't have his phone number."

"So how do you make contact to say you need a visit from women?" George asked.

"There's someone else for that. Well, two of them."

"What are they called? Bear in mind you haven't told us what J's proper name is yet."

"They are HP and M, that's all I'm prepared to say at the minute."

"And you have *their* phone numbers?"

"Yeah, but they change all the time, like they have burners. They use code words to let me know it's them whenever they send me a text from a new number."

George clenched his fists. "And what are they?"

"They call me disciple or watcher, depending on who I am at the time."

George had finished with the biscuits and drank his coffee, leaving Jerry to feel uncomfortable in their silent, brooding presence. Once they'd all drunk up, Jerry announced he was going to go and pack a bag, sounding chipper that he was about to get a free holiday. George didn't want to give him any chance to use his mobile to warn those fuckheads that he was being taken away—he could have been making out he was scared of George and Greg when he wasn't.

"Don't you worry about a bag," George said. "We've got everything you need at the cottage. Tracksuits, toothbrushes, all that sort of thing. I'd leave your phone here if I were you. Who knows whether they've put a tracker on it without your knowledge. Did the police ask to look at it by any chance?"

"I gave them my personal contract phone to nose through—there's sod all on that one. I don't have anything to do with the rituals on there. I use a burner for that, see."

"Leave them both then," George advised.

Jerry took two out of his jeans pockets and laid them on the table, one an old-fashioned thing and another an Apple. "Actually, it'll do me good to have a break from those, not to mention everything else. I have a lot of parties, it pisses the neighbours off, and I've been feeling guilty about it for ages. Maybe going away will give me a chance to sort my head out, see what's missing in my life."

Greg had been using his phone and glanced up from the screen. "Our man will be coming to collect you for us because we have something else we need to do while we're at this end of town."

'Our man' must be Ichabod. George was surprised the Irishman had agreed to help them, because he'd taken a massive step back from the bad side of the business, wanting to be a good boy now his missus had a baby on the way.

"Is he aware of where Jerry needs to go?" George asked, meaning the steel room at the cottage.

Greg nodded. "Why don't you go for a quick piss while you're near a toilet, bruv."

George took the hint to search the house and left the kitchen. Glad there wasn't a loo downstairs, he went up and had a poke around Jerry's bedroom, in his drawers and wardrobe and under the bed, searching for something that would lead to the true identity of the High Priest and this Mocha fella. George wasn't overly bothered about Julian because it sounded like he wasn't one of the string-pullers in this operation but a pawn, just like the women.

He found nothing.

Annoyed, he checked the spare room, which was an office, one of the tidiest he'd ever seen. Again, nothing to report there, so he nipped into the bathroom to flush the toilet, then went back downstairs. Jerry stood near the front door with Greg, the shadow of someone else outside on the path showing through the blurry glass.

He got here quick.

"You have yourself a nice break," George said, intending to give Jerry many breaks, especially on his fingers if he didn't tell them what they wanted to know later on. He wished he could be there to see the bloke's face when he was strung up by Ichabod, but they really needed to nip over and see Sandra, then there were the other neighbours, the biggest culprits in littering the street with fucked-up fridges and shit-stained mattresses outside. There was no fucking need for it, and George was pretty raging about it to be honest.

Greg open the front door to reveal Ichabod in a wig, beard, a flat cap, and a pair of red-framed glasses. He nodded to Jerry in greeting, and the pair of them walked down the path to an SUV that Dwayne, their car thief, had likely parked behind Jackpot Palace, the twins' casino that Ichabod managed. Cars were pinched, stored there for a while until the heat died down, then moved on to a garage that removed all traces of their former origin for them to be sold abroad.

George and Greg left the house and closed the door, Greg slipping a bunch of keys in his pocket, probably so they could send a crew in during the night to ransack the place properly.

Ichabod drove away.

Instead of crossing the street and going straight to Sandra's, because that would be too fucking obvious that she was a snitch, George jerked his head at Greg.

They got in their taxi.

"I thought we were going to see Sandra." Greg drove up the street.

"We are, but we need to go home and change into our leader suits and get these wigs and whatnot off. We'll switch the taxi for the BMW."

"But it's better that we speak to her in disguise."

"Not on this occasion, because I want everybody to see *everyone* being spoken to, not just about what happened last night but about the shit state of that fucking street. It's disgusting and needs sorting."

"What are you going to be saying to the residents?"

"That if they don't clean it up by this time next week, everyone gets their head kicked in, it's as simple as that. We'll go inside a few houses so it doesn't look odd when we go in Sandra's."

Greg nodded and headed in the direction of their place.

Chapter Four

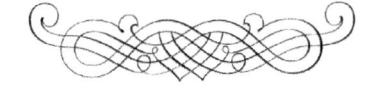

Jerry wasn't fond of the gruff and to-the-point Irishman driving him out into the countryside, but he supposed it didn't matter *what* he felt about him because he was being dropped off at a safe house and would be left to his own devices, so it wasn't as if Jerry had to be best buddies with him, was it. Still, it would have been nice to have a pleasant chat on the journey instead of feeling like he was in the way, as though taking him to a cottage wasn't something Paddy wanted to do.

I bet that's his name.

Jerry held back a chuckle, then he felt bad. If it wasn't for this man, he wouldn't be on his way to safety. He shouldn't be so quick to take the piss. It was nice of the twins to do this for him, you know, keep him out of the way while the police investigated the High Priest and whatever, because he didn't feel safe at all being left at home, not now the pigs had spoken to him. The High Priest might think Jerry had caved under pressure, even though he hadn't that time when he'd been tricked into thinking some thugs had wanted to know all about the rituals.

Jerry had been minding his own business down the boozer, sinking a few pints, not expecting to be waylaid when he'd left. Except he was, down a fucking alley, these two big bastards in balaclavas following him. That was enough to make anyone shit themselves, so he'd run, and then *they'd* run. Next thing he knew, one of them had punched him in the back of the head, and he'd gone flying forward, landing face-first on the tarmac, his nose breaking. The pain of it had been sodding awful, spreading over his whole face and spearing agony into his brain. He'd registered then that his top lip had split, too. He'd gingerly probed at it with his tongue, trying to come to terms with the fact that someone had *actually pushed him over* for no apparent reason, when he'd been hauled to his feet by one of them grabbing the back of his jacket.

He could still see them now, standing between the cones of light from two streetlamps, their shadowy silhouettes against the backdrop of a wooden fence, the whites of their eyes bright in the darkness. They'd asked about the rituals, and he'd made out he didn't know what they were guffing on about. The thugs had given him a couple of thumps to his stomach, saying *they* knew that *he* knew, but he'd maintained his innocence, and eventually they'd fucked off.

He shuddered at the memory of how scared he'd been, and just as he'd stepped out of the alley into the safety of a residential road, the burner phone the High Priest had posted to his house had rung.

"Good man, you passed one of my tests."

"I told you I wouldn't tell anyone about what I pay you for. They broke my fucking *nose*."

"Sorry about that, but I can't guarantee there won't be casualties when my men do their checks."

The line had gone dead, and Jerry had walked home with searing pain in his forehead and nose, his lip throbbing, blood dripping from his nostrils over his mouth. He'd stared into the mirror in his bathroom, shocked at the state of himself, wondering whether this was going to be a regular occurrence, the High Priest continually double-checking whether he was going to give away any secrets. He remembered thinking, staring at his reflection, that this likely wasn't worth all the hassle. But the lure of participating in a sexual ritual was something he'd wanted to do ever since someone had told him about it during one of his house parties. The man had slipped him a number—he'd gate-crashed, now Jerry came to think of it—and he'd phoned it, someone called Mocha answering. After a set of bizarre and pointless questions, Jerry was given another number which happened to be for the High Priest.

The rest was history, but now look, he was being spirited away to safety because his sexual appetite had led him down a path he should never have gone down. Well, the rituals had been okay, it was having women at his house that had gone so wrong. Someone had phoned the police. Jerry could pick any number of neighbours who would've done it. A lot of them had complained about his parties in the past, and he'd been pissed as a fart and told them to fuck off, laughing his head off, telling them to go and get a life, but they'd had the last laugh because the police had wanted to dig into the rituals and everything, asking Jerry questions he wasn't allowed to answer. Who'd told them about everything? That woman who'd legged it out the front?

God, all he wanted to do now was live a quiet life.

That was on offer at the twins' cottage, a nice little getaway where he could reevaluate without any distractions. It was true what he'd said to them, that he ought to sort his life out. He'd been such a dickhead for years and had nothing better to spend his savings on other than paying for girls, when really, he could have paid for a Spanish break instead and got the girls for free.

People still had holiday romances, didn't they?

The Irishman turned down a track, and soon they came to a lovely cottage hidden away amongst the trees. Jerry got out and marvelled at how something so idyllic could exist only a few miles from the hustle and bustle of city life. He'd swear blind he was right in the proper countryside, in Wales or the Lake District, somewhere like that. He felt better already, all that pure fresh air.

"I'll be back in a sec." The Irishman disappeared round the back and returned holding a set of keys. "I'll give ye a quick tour."

Jerry turned to him and nodded, letting him lead the way. Inside, they stood in a small hallway, a couple of closed doors nearby. He was ushered forward to a locked door ahead. That was a bit odd, it being locked, but maybe it was for a private suite. Maybe there were suites behind the *other* doors, too. It made sense to maximise the profit of renting it out.

Door open, Jerry was about to step inside when the metal decor and a table with tools on top gave him pause. A whack to the back of the head brought on déjà vu, except this time he fell onto a steel floor rather than tarmac.

What the *fuck* was going on?

Chapter Five

*V*ee looked down the road to her right from the top of the T-junction where she stood. This was an industrial estate with only a few streetlamps shining, ominous patches of blackness between that held shadows and ghosts. All the businesses were closed at this time of night, hence why the sex workers had chosen this spot to tout their wares once it got dark.

Trees bordered the top of the T in both directions, and from where she stood, the two routes away from here were completely black apart from a lamppost or two farther along. From what she'd gathered when working on the case, at home time the women had walked from here, down the T top, then around the corner behind the industrial estate to the nearby housing estate, which was still too far away for people to hear if anyone screamed, but close enough to run to if someone needed help.

Put simply, the area was creepy and desolate.

Vee stood all alone, or that's what it felt like, but one of her colleagues had parked between a carpet shop and Kwik Fit, while some stood on the other side of the T top behind the trees, a farmer's field beyond. Even though they were there, she still felt vulnerable and imagined what it must have been like for the sex workers. She was surprised they'd come here in the first place—it was so eerie—but at least with the abductions they'd buggered off elsewhere.

The sound of a car engine drew her attention down the T top behind her. Headlights lit up the night, on full beam so she had to squint. The vehicle slowed as it drove past her, and her stomach rolled over at the thought of the abductors being inside, checking to see if she was their type. She couldn't be that that lucky, could she, for them to appear tonight, her first stint on the corner?

The car stopped, reversed to her, and she took in its details to file them in her memory: Audi, dark, new registration plate, slightly tinted windows. The one on the driver's side sailed down, and a smiling face appeared in the gap.

"How much, love?" the man asked.

Brown hair. In his forties. Acne scars on his cheeks. A strange little what's-the-point beard that was too patchy to be anything but bumfluff. Hazel eyes that appeared kind, a wrinkle or two beside them. He didn't seem to be anyone to worry about, but not all kidnappers had stone-cold glares and hardened features. Some looked like your best mate. He, however, didn't match Tara's descriptions of Mocha and Julian.

"Sorry, I'm just off home."

Taylor had dismissed the idea of officers approaching any suspects as soon as they stopped, his excuse being that if the abductor didn't talk down at the station, and the women had been locked in that house, then how could they be saved? Everyone had agreed that following the vehicle was the better, if more risky, option.

"That's a shame." He smiled. "Another time, maybe."

The window went up, and he drove away. Anxiety gave Vee a big prod in the stomach, twisting it into knots and sending her legs a little weak—had she been that close to being taken? She knew damn well that's why she was there, and she expected to be abducted, but what she hadn't *expected was to feel so scared once he was gone.*

She'd realised the enormity of it, that was it. Shit. Was she really the best person for this? Should she give one of the many signals the team had discussed and call it off? Let someone else deal with this? Had she just sent the abductor away, or was he an innocent punter? She wished she had her police earpiece in so she could listen to any feedback regarding the Audi—someone in the team would already be putting it through the database to see who owned it—but an earpiece would give her away if anyone saw it.

It was bad enough she had a phone in her knickers.

She stared ahead at the taillights, two red devil eyes. They got smaller and smaller, and he didn't turn off onto the Bradwell housing estate like she'd expected but kept going. She spun back the other way at the sound of another engine, her nerves shot. A Kia, red with a black stripe down the side, nothing like the abductor's vehicle. It went by, and she relaxed a tad, but her heartbeat kept soaring. She counted to ten, then backwards, several times to calm herself down.

She spent the next fifteen minutes stomping her feet trying to keep warm.

Then another engine.

Once again, she turned to watch a vehicle approach, and her instinct told her she'd got lucky—or should that be unlucky now she was having second thoughts about taking on this role? A dark SUV, something Tara had mentioned. The type that had two rows of seats in the back. Vee slapped on a smile and waited for the driver to stop and lower his window. He did, but only by a couple of inches, so all she could see were his eyes through the slit and white skin, thick eyebrows, a close-cropped hairline.

"Are you for sale?" he asked, his voice rough as if he smoked too many cigarettes.

She nodded. "Yes."

"Get in the back."

Was this the man they were looking for? Was this what he'd done with the other women, ordering them into the back? Technically that wouldn't be kidnap, but keeping them in the house with the boarded-up windows was.

"Err, hold your horses a sec. Tell me what you're after first," she said.

"No sex, just a chat."

She laughed to make out she'd heard that one before. "Like I'm going to believe that."

"My wife doesn't understand me," he said, the skin beside his eyes moving, indicating he might be smiling.

"That's what they all say." She smiled back and partially twisted away from him to make out she wasn't interested.

"Look, I'll give you half now and half afterwards." He held some money out of the gap in the window. Two fifty-pound notes flapped in the breeze.

"What do you want to talk about?" she asked. "I need to know before I get in your car."

"Just stuff. Life."

Thinking of what Taylor would want her to do, and considering this was an SUV with two sets of rear doors, she shrugged and got in, tamping down the jolt of fear when she discovered someone else was already sitting there. A brown-haired woman with a blindfold on.

She stuffed her worry away. "Hey, I'm not into kinky shit; no threesomes or anything." Vee went to back out.

A door shutting. Footsteps.

Before she had time to react, someone pushed her from behind and stuffed her inside the vehicle.

Whoever it was must have been sitting in the passenger seat and she hadn't spotted them through that small slit in the driver's window. The team would likely be taking pictures with their flashes off. Was this another woman or a man? The door closed, slamming onto her feet and sending her face-first into the woman's lap. Vee scrabbled upright and went to open the door to escape, to make out she was a genuine victim and not a copper — she seriously fucking wished she hadn't agreed to be the bait, but it was too late now.

She sat up just as the SUV sped off. She caught sight of a colleague peering from behind one of the trees and giving her the 'okay' sign. It wasn't okay, she should have kept out of this and stayed at home with another HelloFresh dinner.

"Just sit still and quiet," the woman whispered. "And put this on."

She held out a blindfold. Vee took it, but before she put it on, she looked at the front passenger. A man with a balaclava on. She swallowed a glut of trepidation and lowered the material over her eyes, although she left enough of a gap to still see out of the side.

"Put it on properly, you fucking whore," the driver said, and the door locks clunked.

Vee did as she was told — it was fine, a team member would be following, but that didn't mean she wasn't shitting herself. She'd known about the blindfold from Tara, had expected it, had known damn well she'd be prevented from seeing where she was going, but to actually go through it was more unnerving than she'd imagined.

This is your job. Get on with it.

"Where are we going for this 'chat'?" she asked.

"To the house," a man said. It sounded like the driver again.

"Well, if we're going to become friends, what's your name?"

"Mocha."

"Why are you called that?"

"Because I like chocolate coffee, you dumb bitch."

"Fucking hell, keep your hair on, I only asked." Vee tutted to let him think she thought he was just a customer, even though it was clear that wasn't the case, considering there was a passenger at the front and another in the back. "If you just want to talk, how come you've got your mates with you?"

"Jesus, just shut your cakehole, woman."

"What if I don't want to?" *She was pushing it but needed to get a rise out of him so he showed her who he really was—what he really wanted.*

"Then I'll slit your throat so you can't speak ever again. Now be quiet, you're getting on my tits."

"You're mad to be saying this shit to me when the twins run the Estate," she said. "You do realise most of the sex workers on Cardigan are protected by them, right? If I go back and tell them what you said..."

"I'm not bothered about those two cunts. Now like I said, be quiet."

"What about this chat?"

"Fuck me, lady. We'll have it at my gaff, all right?"

"Fair enough."

She settled onto the seat to play the game, although it was bugging her she couldn't see anything. A hand rested on her leg and patted. Vee assumed the woman had done it to comfort her. There had been no time for Vee to get a good look at her—was she one of the other abducted women the team knew about? Or one they didn't? Or was she someone who'd also been taken off the street this evening?

"We're being followed," Mocha said. "Whip the gun out and get rid of them."

Vee's stomach rolled over. It would be one of her team. What if they got shot? There was no way she could take the burner phone out of her knickers to contact Taylor without being seen, so she couldn't warn him. She had no choice but to let this play out. Many scenarios had been accounted for, or at least this one had, so whoever followed in the unmarked police car would have a contingency plan if a gun appeared out of one of the windows.

A cold blast of air barged in and tossed Vee's hair around. Thank God she hadn't put on a short skirt but leggings. Her thin imitation leather jacket wasn't doing much to keep the chill away, though, so she rubbed her arms and shouted, "Bloody Nora, can you shut that window?"

"Just be quiet," the other woman said. "Please. It's for your own good."

"Why are we being followed?" Vee asked, injecting a shot of panic into her voice.

Mocha piped up with: "Didn't I fucking say we shouldn't come back down here? Didn't I warn you the place might be being watched?"

"But we never saw anyone," the front passenger said—a male.

"That car behind us came out of the industrial estate," Mocha shouted.

"So? It could be someone working late. What if I shoot an innocent person?"

The movement of the vehicle changed, flinging Vee into the door beside her, her arm bashing into it, then the SUV went the other way so she leaned against the woman.

"Put the gun away," Mocha said. *"Whoever it is isn't even copying what I'm doing."*

Vee wanted to snipe that this wasn't a TV programme, any normal person driving behind a car didn't generally mimic the person in front's actions. The breeze stopped, so she assumed the window had gone up and the danger had passed.

"We'll drive around the housing estate, go in from the top end, and if we're still followed, then we know the score."

"You said the least amount of people who see the car, the better, yet you want to drive about?" the other man said.

"That was before we had someone right up our arse, you prick."

"So what do you want me to do, shoot them out of the window on a bloody housing estate, because I'm not doing that."

"You'll do whatever I say, Julian."

Vee took note of that name — it was the same one Tara had told her, the man who looked after the abducted women in the boarded-up house. He was kind and seemed forced into doing his job — Tara had sworn blind Mocha had something on Julian, some sort of secret.

Maybe if I can get close to him, get him to trust me, Julian will open up.

Vee lifted her hand to scratch the back of her head, a prearranged signal to the officer following that she'd discovered they were on the right track and with the right people. On her first night on the job, she'd been picked up by the abductors—what were the odds?

She scratched her head for a good while then lowered her hand to her lap, wishing she could take the burner phone out of her knickers and send Taylor a message, but she couldn't. Going by the amount of time she'd already spent in the car and it turning right, she gathered they were now on the Bradwell housing estate. She knew this place well so counted each turn left and right until she was convinced they were on Goldcrest Way where those big houses were.

The SUV moved on after a pause, going faster, and Vee worked out that they'd come out on the other side of the housing estate and were on the main road.

What if they were on the way to the stones' location?

All this time Vee had assumed she'd be taken straight to the house and introduced to any other women the same as Tara had been, then she'd be taught what she had to do on the stones with those creepy men.

But what if that wasn't going to happen?

What if Vee was thrust straight into one of those rituals?

Chapter Six

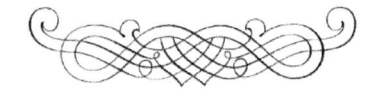

Mr Tarquin Roberts had gained a bit of a name for himself over the years, acting like a knobhead for the majority of the time and generally giving people grief. Wankers like that pissed George the fuck off, and when he'd been going out during the night as his alter ego, Ruffian, Tarquin's type were his main targets.

There was nothing better than wiping smug smirks off the faces of people who thought they were untouchable.

When the man in question opened his front door and saw the twins standing there, George thought the resident would have made the decision to rein in any stupid words that had a mind to come out of his mouth. Unfortunately for him, he hadn't, and it had resulted in George punching him in the face and giving him a fat lip. The resulting swelling and bruising was pleasing to the eye, and talking of eyes, Tarquin's were leaking something chronic. Pain had a habit of doing that to you, making them water, but he was crying.

George smiled as though he had all the patience in the world, when actually, today it was thinner than any other day he could remember. He'd had times where it was this thin, but not when it was accompanied with immense irritation, the type that felt like sandpaper abraded his nerves, or as if he'd woken up grumpy because something had happened in a dream that had set him off.

"Now then, I'll ask again, sunshine. When are you going to be clearing up this mess in your front garden?"

George gave it another gander. As far as he could make out, you could furnish a room with this load of bollocks. The rolled-up rug appeared to have been there since the last century. All right, an exaggeration, but it was filthy. The fucker was so rotten that the backing had deteriorated over time, been gnawed on by mice or rats, something George did *not* want to encounter while he stood on this prick's garden path, but if he did, then Tarquin would pay for it.

"Today." Tarquin winced at his sore lip. "I'll get down the tip an' that."

"Make sure you do it before your lip grows too big for you to see over it." George chuckled at his own joke. "That fridge there looks like it's going to walk off by itself because I'll bet it's alive with shit inside."

"This isn't *Beauty and the Beast*," Tarquin said.

"Am I supposed to have found that funny?" George asked.

"Well, it's got animated furniture in it and stuff, and you said the fridge might walk—"

"Shut up, please, just shut up, or I'll have to make you. Let us in so we can look at the back garden. If the front's anything to go by, then I dread to think what we're going to see."

Tarquin looked as though he was about to kick up a fuss but thought better of it and led them through the house to the kitchen. Every now and again he raised his hand to his face, probably touching his lip. He leaned against the worktop with his arms folded, his chin sporting a purple bruise that had come on pretty quickly.

George peered through the glass in the back door and frowned. The interior of the house and the back garden were pristine, a far cry from what he'd expected. Why the hell was the front so gopping?

"Why give the impression that you live in a shithole when you don't?" he asked.

Tarquin smiled. "Tactical move, innit. If people think you're a dirty fucking bastard, they won't rob you."

"I can see your logic, but there's no need to go to the degree you have. You've got a whole room's worth of furniture out there in various stages of decay. I want it gone. Invest in home security if you're worried about break-ins. You know, cameras and video doorbells."

They left the house and at last headed to Sandra's. George had spotted her watching them from her living room on several occasions in the past half an hour while they'd been at front doors. Greg tapped on hers, and she answered, her expression one of concern that the twins were on her doorstep—all done for her neighbours' benefit.

"Can I help you?" she said, perfectly playing her part of not working for them.

"We're here on a mission to get the street cleaned up," George said. "I can see the front of yours is absolutely fine, but we need to come and see the back. The council are shocking, they're not making residents look after the properties, and this street is nothing but an eyesore."

She stepped back to let them in, and after closing the door said, "Something went on over the road last night. I only found out about it a little while ago because we've had a lie-in this morning. It's my youngest's birthday. Me and Sally were up last night blowing up balloons and getting things ready. When we finally finished and went and had a cuppa in the living room, I didn't have my curtains shut. We saw a car turn up opposite. I assumed it was a taxi. Some people got out of it, and I told my Sally that Jerry must be having one of his parties. We decided to get to bed before the music started, because it's a bugger to get to sleep if it's on before you manage to nod off. Anyway, like I said, we slept in, and I've not long had her next door come round and tell me the police were in the street during the night, no idea what for, though. I was about to let you know when I saw you turn up. Do you want a coffee?"

Take a fucking breath, love. "Only if you've bought a nice machine recently."

"One arrived this morning as it happens. That's what got me out of bed, the Amazon driver knocking."

"What sort did you get?" Greg asked.

"A Tassimo, like George suggested. No idea how to work it."

"Did you get any pods with it?"

"I did."

"Then I'll set it up for you and show you what's what while we have a chat."

They trooped into the kitchen, Greg taking charge of pulling the machine out of the box and placing it on the side. Sandra watched him.

"These parties Jerry has," George said. "Have you ever been to one?"

"No I bleedin' haven't. It's usually all women who turn up, which I find a bit odd, don't you? I mean, there's his age for a start; everyone who goes there is so much younger."

"Do you know him well?"

"No."

"So you don't know anything about rituals and high priests?"

"No! I mean, what do you think I'm on?"

George smiled.

The thumping of footsteps on the stairs and a massive shriek drew his attention to the door. Two small kids flew down the hallway.

"Happy birthday!" Sandra shouted and crouched with her arms out.

One of the children flew into them. "Can I have my presents now?"

"Go and wake Sally up first so we can all watch you open them."

It was clear Sandra didn't know anything of interest regarding Jerry, but that didn't mean her eldest daughter, Sally, didn't have any snippets. While Sandra went off into the living room to wait for all of her kids, George stared out into the back garden at the manky old swing set. It must have belonged to Sally at one time a couple of decades ago. Even though they paid Sandra a fair whack for her snooping services, he made a mental note to get some new play equipment delivered. It was the kid's birthday, after all.

More footsteps came, one set lighter than the other, then some more, slower, probably Sally. She glanced into the kitchen at them, nodded, then joined her family in the living room. Greg paused in setting up the Tassimo machine, and for a moment they sat at the table listening to the sounds of happiness and the tearing of wrapping paper being stripped off of boxes

Ten minutes later, Sally came in. "Mum whispered that you need to know about Jerry. What kind of thing?"

"Anything that's a bit off," George said.

"There were a couple of times when he left the house in the evenings wearing a red cloak, and another few I saw him in a black one—weirdo. He got in a taxi. I couldn't tell you what company it was, though, but it wasn't a black cab. It was white with a logo on the door in blue. I remember that time was Valentine's Day last year because there were roses on the parcel shelf. I saw them when the driver went off, like he'd put fake ones there for the day."

"That's actually a massive help," George said. "Thank you. Anything else?"

"Only that he has parties and loads of young girls there."

"Okay, cheers. Tell your mum we'll see ourselves out and for her to expect a delivery later this afternoon."

George led the way out of the house and, in the BMW, he sent a message to Will, asking him to order a wooden jungle gym with a slide and swings attached, plus a little house the kiddies could use as a den. Then he messaged their private detective, Mason.

GG: NEED YOU TO RING ALL TAXI FIRMS AND FIND OUT WHERE THIS BLOKE WAS DROPPED OFF. RELEVANT INFO: JERRY WATSON, 4 ALDING CLOSE, WEARING A RED OR BLACK CLOAK, VALENTINE'S DAY 2024.

MASON: ON IT.

Greg got in the car. "You didn't give me a chance to show Sandra how to work the machine, you plonker."

"There's instructions."

Greg snapped his seat belt on. "Why the rush?"

"I've got Mason working on finding out where Jerry was taken on the night he used the white taxi. For all we know it could have been to the High Priest's house or the one where Fantasy was kept."

"If he was wearing cloaks, it'll more than likely turn out to be sites for the rituals. Fantasy said they changed locations each week, so knowing them isn't going to be any good to us."

"I still need to feel like I'm *doing* something. Right, we'll go to the cottage. Jerry's had long enough to hang there and have a good think. Hopefully he'll be ready to talk by the time we arrive."

"And if he isn't?"

"I can't believe you're asking me that. What do I usually do when people don't talk?"

"Hmm. What's your objective here?"

"Believe it or not, I want to know the address of the boarded-up house more than anything so we can rescue the other women—from what we've been told, that undercover copper is just as trapped as Pearl and Candy."

Colin had told them the planned abduction of Vee had gone wrong, and the police team in the car following the SUV had lost the targets on a housing estate.

George shook his head about that. "Once we've paid the house a visit, if we ever find out where it is, we can speak to Julian and Mocha. Maybe they know where the High Priest lives."

"Right." Greg drove away. "But if it's like Fantasy said, they won't know anything."

George stared out of the windscreen, wishing he'd gone to town on Tarquin to get some of the tension out of his bones. The way he felt at the moment, he'd launch an attack on Jerry the second he saw him, and that wasn't wise.

Information first, death later.

Chapter Seven

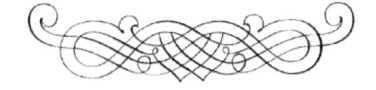

It felt weird being in the cottage now that they'd agreed not to use it to harbour any more dead bodies—not that they were doing that this time. George had planned to keep this place as somewhere to torture people, somewhere they could be left unattended where no one would hear them calling out, but like a kid with a new toy, he now favoured using the cellar in their latest warehouse which had a trapdoor in the floor that opened up to the gushing Thames beneath.

"Ah, it's good to be back." George entered the cottage and sniffed, wanting to make sure the stench of the rotten bodies beneath the steel door really *was* gone. He couldn't detect anything but a nearby Febreze plug-in, so he nodded to himself and walked down the hallway and round the corner to the kitchen.

Seeing as they hadn't had a coffee at Sandra's, he fancied one now, not to mention something to eat. They'd left home without having any breakfast, shooting off to speak to Fantasy, then going to Alding Close and spending far too long there for his liking (but at the same time he'd wanted to deal with it there and then so it wasn't on his mind later). He made coffee and placed the cups on the table. A quick look at their phone revealed that Colin had got back with a few more titbits.

COLIN: JERRY'S GOT A CLEAN RECORD. HE WAS A WITNESS IN A FIGHT IN TOWN TEN YEARS AGO WHERE SOMEONE WAS KICKED IN THE HEAD AND DIED. HE WAS NOTHING TO DO WITH THE ATTACK, AND FROM

WHAT I CAN GATHER FROM THE REPORT, HE WAS COOPERATIVE AS A WITNESS.

George paused to digest that information, then continued reading the second text.

COLIN: HOWEVER, THERE ARE SEVERAL REPORTS OF DISTURBANCES WHERE HE'S HELD PARTIES AT HIS HOUSE. SOME PEOPLE STATED HE'S NOT SO NICE WHEN HE'S GOT THE DRINK IN HIM. SEEMS TO THINK IT'S HIS RIGHT TO HOLD LOUD PARTIES WHENEVER HE WANTS TO, ALTHOUGH HE HAS LOWERED THE MUSIC AFTER THE POLICE HAVE VISITED.

GG: CHEERS.

George thought Jerry was just one of those twats every street had, but then your average twat didn't put on a cloak, dance around stones to weird music, and treat women like they were worthless, did they. He'd bet there was more to Jerry than met the eye, and after this short break, he'd go and find out.

"What's your take on him?" George asked his brother.

"Bit of a pervert, probably lonely, acts like a knob as a way to hide his real feelings, which are probably of inadequacy and self-loathing."

George nodded. "I agree. He shouldn't be too difficult to crack."

George made them both a chicken and mushroom Pot Noodle (no tiger bread, which dogged him off), and they ate in silence. George went through the questions he would be asking Jerry, cementing them in his mind. With his hunger kept at bay for now, they put on their forensic gear and unlocked the door to the steel room.

George poked his head round the edge. "*There* you are!"

Jerry whimpered. "Oh, thank God! That man, he brought me here and strung me up! Punched me in the face to knock me to the floor first. I knew there was a reason I didn't like him in the car."

George moved into the room a bit more to allow Greg to come in. "You say that as though I didn't give him permission to do it. I'm *sure* one of us said you'd be hanging around here."

"Yeah, but not like this!" Jerry, naked and with a shrivelled cock from the cold or fear, puffed out so much air his bottom lip wobbled. "Please get me down, my armpits are hurting."

"Tell me what we need to know—all of it."

"I might not *know* all of it. Bloody hell, I've got no idea where the girls live, I don't know where *any* of them live."

"That's a shame. Tell me something I can use to work out how to find them, because I'm telling you, there's no way those rituals and sex nights ought to be happening on our Estate. I want them stopped—*and* the people who're organising them."

It seemed Jerry had realised he was better off talking. "Okay, okay, you know I said Mocha gave me the High Priest's number? Well, when I rang it, I had to give him my name so he could do a security check on me. That's what he said anyway. A burner phone arrived in the post, and there was already a message on it, which was for me to go to a pub and wait round the back."

"What pub?"

"The Cricketer's Arms down Fold Street. The back of it's on a road where there are these buildings opposite, they look like they might be offices. So I waited there, in the dark, and then this car comes along. A black SUV, the sort that has like six seats in the back, so six doors, seven if you include the boot."

"Do you remember the licence plate?"

"No. So it parked, and this skinny bloke got out. He had this white plastic face mask on, and the hood of his sweatshirt was up, so I couldn't even see what colour hair or eyebrows he had. He said the security check had come back okay, the same with the credit scoring so he knew I was good for paying my bills and stuff. Oh, and I forgot to say that the message also told me to bring five thousand quid in cash, in an envelope, which was the payment for my first few rituals."

"Where the fuck did you get that kind of money from?"

"I've been single for years so I'd saved loads."

"What happened then?"

"He said I had to follow him to this place and that my first ritual was that night. I remember it was a Saturday, they were always held on a Saturday, and it bothered me that I hadn't had a chance to have a shower an' that—the stupid shit you think about, eh? I kept thinking I didn't have time to prepare, because I like to mull things over before I actually do them. I mean, it's not like I hadn't imagined doing something like that before because I had, which was why I wanted to do the ritual in the first place, but to actually have it dumped on me was a bit of a shock. Maybe it had to be done that way so I didn't have a chance to tell anyone what I was doing, which to be fair is a good idea, because as soon as I'd participated in a ritual, I knew I'd never tell anyone because I didn't want to be stopped from doing it again. Kind of like he had me hook, line, and sinker."

"Where was it held?"

"The first one was in Daffodil Woods, and there haven't been any up there since. They don't repeat locations. I don't know if that's true because I haven't been to every single Saturday night; it's too expensive. When you sign up you have to agree to do five at the very least. And that was all I was prepared to spend—to begin with anyway."

"That's an expensive hobby."

"Yeah, and it's addictive, so when they told me the rituals were over, I was really upset."

"Did they say why they were over?"

"No."

"Tell us about that first night."

"So I had to park my car in this clearing with some others, right, and he put his SUV there, too."

"Did you take any notice of the number plate?"

"No. Have you been to those woods before?"

"Yep."

"Then you know the actual car park at the top of the track? We didn't park there, we had to turn right down the middle pathway and the opening was down there. He gave me this black cloak and told me to put it on as well as one of those white masks. It scared me a bit but at the same time it was exciting. It was all a bit much to take in because, like I said, I prefer to think about things before I do them. It was like I had too much information hit me at once."

"That's terrible for you…"

The sarcasm didn't appear to hit its intended target.

Jerry continued his story. "It was, I can tell you. There were some other men there, at the backs of their cars by their boots. I recognised a couple of them as they took their cloaks out of their holdalls—once you're given a cloak then it's yours to keep. The High Priest said he doesn't want to wash it after we've done what we've done in them."

"Too much information."

"Sorry. So the men, they're obviously getting ready, and they looked over at me, and I felt really exposed, the new kid. Maybe they were worrying that I'd seen their faces, because I hadn't had the speech yet about keeping shit to myself, I hadn't been threatened by that point. I can see it now that the High Priest wanted to get me hooked before he gave me all the rules."

"So who were these other men?"

"One of them was an MP, and the other was some councillor I'd seen on the news. They didn't seem bothered I'd clocked their faces, like they believed the High Priest when he said they were protected. He told me I was protected, too, and I was 'one of them' now."

"What were their names?"

"Oliver Prendergast and Gideon Mainwaring."

"Fuck me, even their names speak of privilege." George had heard of both of them, although the councillor, Gideon, lived on the Proust Estate.

Now he wanted to get inside Jerry's head to see if participating in the rituals made him feel a different kind of person, like when George slipped into his Ruffian persona. This wasn't so he could have common ground with the bloke, he just needed to understand.

"How did you feel when you put on the mask and cloak?"

"Part of me was excited, because I belonged to something, something bigger than anything I'd ever done before, and it was weird that someone like me was mixing with people like them. I never thought that would happen in my lifetime, that when the mask and cape went on, we were equals. It just goes to show that so long as you can afford to pay for a service then it doesn't matter who you are. I'll admit I felt better about myself, as if being accepted into this inner circle with its secrets and whatever, I finally belonged or had been accepted. Maybe not accepted, actually, because common sorts like me are never welcomed by posh buggers like them. Fucking stupid when you think about it, how I'd tried to fool myself, because all the High Priest ever wanted was my money, but for a little while I believed he actually cared about me, that he *wanted* me in his group."

What was it about humans needing to be accepted that they'd do unspeakable things in order to fit in? George would never get it, because he'd always had his twin, so he'd never been lonely and he'd always belonged. He tried to put himself in Jerry's shoes but failed.

"I take it the time you've had to think while you've been hanging here has made you realise a few things. Like how naive you were. How needy."

Jerry winced. "No need to be so blunt, is there?"

"I prefer being blunt. Earlier on at your house, you said you didn't know the women didn't get paid, and I believe you. Since you've had some time to reflect, how do you feel about that now?"

"I don't know. All I wanted was to get off, and as far as I was concerned, so long as it was paid for, then I'd done my bit. What happened to the money after I'd handed it over wasn't any of my business, and I see now that I should have been more interested in what was going on."

"You got carried away with the excitement, didn't you."

"We all did. During the ritual, we were in charge of the women, or that's what it felt like, and they were nothing but puppets. I dig that kind of thing, know what I mean?"

"No, I don't. What else can you tell us about the High Priest?"

"He meets Mocha at the Cricketer's Arms. I overheard them talking once. I don't think I was supposed to know that."

"Did they ever say how often they met there?"

"No, just that it was evenings and they had to wear their masks. Can I get down now? I've told you all I know. That horrible Irishman, that Paddy, he said you were going to kill me. I did what you wanted, so please, please, I won't tell anyone what we talked about. I'll move away and never come back."

"I need you to stay there for a little while longer, possibly overnight, it depends how far we get in our investigation, not only into you but into the others. See you when we see you."

George ignored the man's wailing and walked out, his twin following. Greg locked the door, and they went into the kitchen to take their outfits off.

"Why didn't you just kill him?" Greg asked. "He's useless to us now, and it's too dangerous to let him go back home. He'll tell the first person who'll listen what happened here. Plus, I told Ichabod not to bother with a blindfold because I thought he'd be dead by now, so Jerry knows exactly where this place is."

"I just like the idea of leaving him hanging there overnight because we can. I want him to feel like the women did when they were lying on those stones—exposed, ready to be pounced on at any minute. Scared. He hasn't got a clue whether we'll leave him there for hours or whether we'll go back in and torture him. That's what I want him to feel, unsure."

"Fair enough. Who do you want to see first, the MP or the councillor?"

"The councillor, but we need to get changed into disguises for that, and in the meantime, I'll get Colin to look into where the blokes are at the moment. Then I need to send our Mr Moody into the Cricketer's Arms to have a listen. We might get lucky and someone could drop either Mocha's or the High Priest's name into a conversation."

While Greg drove, George got on with sending the messages.

Chapter Eight

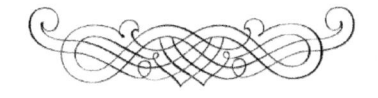

The SUV stopped. Vee held her breath and listened to the noises around her. Car doors opening. Footsteps. She couldn't pick up any strains of the weird music Tara had described, but that didn't mean she hadn't been brought to the fake stone circle. The music might not have started yet; the 'red disciples', as

the women were supposed to call them, might not have arrived.

"You can take the blindfold off now and get out," Mocha said.

Vee did as she was told and stared through the windscreen. A house stood ahead, no lights shining from within. Relief lit her up—she'd been bought to the place with the boarded-up windows, although from the outside it looked like wooden shutters had been placed against the glass on the inside. To anyone driving by it would appear to be an ordinary home.

She got out of the vehicle and glanced around to get her bearings. She had to do it quickly so it didn't look like she was scoping out the surroundings. The place was in the middle of nowhere, of course it bloody was; nothing but the broccoli shapes of trees to the sides and back of the property. The long driveway led to a road, also bordered by trees, no headlights or taillights in sight. In the distance sparkled what she assumed were the lights of the Cardigan Estate or maybe another part of London. The man in the balaclava stood beside the door, hiding something on the wall behind him. Was it a door number, something that would give the location away?

Where were her colleagues in the car that had followed? Mocha and Julian hadn't spoken about it *ever since they'd left what she'd thought was Goldcrest Way — had the drive through the housing estate meant the officer had lost sight of the SUV? The breeze hadn't come in, so the window hadn't been opened again, and there had been no bang of a gunshot.*

Vee didn't know which colleague/s had been placed in the police car, but she had a horrible feeling in the pit of her stomach to go with the horrible thought she'd just had. What if the police in the car happened to be in with Mocha and Julian and had deliberately let the SUV go? No, that was stupid. She'd known everyone on the team for years and trusted them all.

So why had that thought come? Was it panic playing tricks on her?

"Stop gawping and get in the fucking house." Mocha grabbed the top of her arm, digging his fingertips in and wrenching her towards the property.

Vee stumbled along beside him, the other woman on his right-hand side. She appeared to be happy enough to do as she was told and didn't seem like she was going to dart off any second. That married with the statement Tara had given — everyone had been sufficiently frightened enough to obey without question. Or so Mocha and Julian had thought. Tara had just pretended, biding her time until she could run, but she'd mentioned a gun, not that she'd seen one, just that they'd been told they'd be shot if they ran.

Julian took off his balaclava. He brought a set of keys out of his trouser pocket and handed them to Mocha who opened the door. Julian still shielded whatever was on the wall. No shaft of light spilled out into the dark, and as they proceeded into a hallway, she was oddly grateful that Mocha held her arm so she didn't slip or bump into anything. He kicked the front door closed behind them then guided her onwards. Julian and the woman went through another doorway ahead, and a light flicked on.

"Go and sit down." In a kitchen, Mocha gave Vee a shove towards a black dining table with grey velvet carver chairs around it. "Then we can have that chat." He slapped the other woman's bum. "Get the kettle on."

He sat opposite Vee. Julian closed the kitchen door and leaned his back against it. Vee had a good look around—Mocha was too busy picking at his fingernails to start the promised conversation, and Julian stared at the floor. Both men were in their twenties.

She'd been right, there were shutters on the insides of the windows but not the kind that could be opened—they had screws in them. The kitchen was like anyone *else's with a kettle and a coffeemaker on the side, a washing-up bowl in the sink, and a microwave next to a toaster. It was like Tara had said: everyone was told to live here as though it were their own house. Vee checked out the corners of the ceiling where Tara had told her the cameras were. They weren't discreet, perhaps a deliberate visual warning to the women that they were being watched. There weren't any in the other parts of the house, not that Tara had seen anyway.*

"What happened to the car following us?" Vee asked.

"We lost them," Mocha said, "not that it's any of your business."

"Why are you being so snotty? You asked me to get in the car so you could have a chat, but it doesn't mean you have to be rude, does it?"

Mocha smiled at her. "Seeing as I've brought you here to work for our boss, you don't have a say in the matter."

"I bloody well do," she said.

"You've got no handbag," he pointed out, "and there are no bulges in your jacket pockets, so it doesn't appear that you have a phone on you in order to tell someone all about what I've just said, which is a bit fucking stupid, considering the job you do—no phone

when you go off with fuck knows who? Which reminds me, Fantasy will need to pat you down."

Vee assumed that was the other woman's name because she turned from putting the kettle on its base and gestured for Vee to stand. She patted her all over and didn't pause nor flinch when she felt the phone in the front of Vee's knickers, returning to the kettle and taking cups from the cupboard above it afterwards as if nothing had happened.

Vee got slammed with a realisation—Fantasy wasn't any of the three women who'd been reported missing from that corner; she didn't match any of the photos on the interactive board. So where had she been picked up? And were the three abducted women in this house?

"You can sit," Mocha said. "Tell me, what kind of woman goes to work on a street corner without a phone?"

"I was in a rush and left it at home," she said.

"Bad luck for you, good luck for me."

"So this chat…"

"You're going to live here with three other girls and participate in the rituals."

"The rituals?" She knew damn well what they were but had to appear clueless.

Mocha stroked his clean-shaven chin. "You'll find out soon enough. We did have another woman, but the silly fucking slag got away."

Tara.

"You say she got away. That makes it sound like she was here against her will."

"She was. Jesus Christ, are you a div or something?"

"No, I was just making sure I understood what you said. So if I don't agree to work for you doing whatever these rituals are, what happens then?"

"I beat the shit out of you until you agree." He laughed, throwing his head back. "And if you still say no, I'll have to shoot you."

"How much will I get paid?"

He stared at her. "Nothing. The payment is you being grateful to be kept alive. You get food and board, all your clothes bought for you. You don't need any more than that."

Fantasy turned from putting teabags in the cups. "Am I allowed to talk to her?" she asked Mocha.

"Yeah, go on then."

Fantasy smiled at Vee. "It's better if you don't fight it. Just accept you live and work here now, then you won't get hurt."

Vee wasn't sure which way she should play it. Two scenarios had been discussed at the work meeting: she either fought it like the average woman would or she pretended to be submissive and accept her lot. Personally, she thought accepting it would make her look more suspicious, so she pushed her chair back, the legs scraping on the lino, and made a dash for the boarded-up back door. She wrenched on the handle but of course couldn't get outside.

No one took any notice of her, but she carried on regardless, yanking and yanking until she screamed in fake frustration and went down on her knees to cry.

"They're all the fucking same," Mocha said.

"You've never, ever given them a chance to come to terms with all this," Julian said. "You drop it on them like a sack of shit and expect them to be okay with it. If you'd just be more gentle or care *more…"*

"What the fuck do I want to care *for? No one cares about my part in this!" Mocha shook his head. "You're a dick for discussing this in front of them, so shut your gob." He looked at Vee. "And you, get your arse up off the floor, you daft bint."*

She rose and sat at the table, wiping tears from her hot face and smiling her thanks at Fantasy who put a cup of tea in front of her. Vee waited for Fantasy to go back to collect another cup for Mocha so the woman was out of the way, then she threw her scalding drink towards his face. He must have expected it because he darted to the right and the tea landed on his shoulder, sliding down his leather jacket.

"Can you make another cuppa, please," he said casually—he actually sounded weary, bored. "This silly cow's gone and spilled hers." He narrowed his eyes at Vee. "I'm a patient man, but it's wearing thin. If you do that again, I'll break the cup and ram the shard right up your cunt."

He'd said it with such venom she believed him.

"I'm not sorry," she whispered.

"You will be if you carry on. Now then, calm your tits and listen to what I've got to say. If you're good, I'll let you meet the other women tonight. If you're not, you'll be put in the old laundry room."

Tara had been placed there as a punishment once or twice, and because Vee was desperate to meet the other women and see who she could trust to get an escape plan together, she had no inclination to spend the night in the black-walled room, chained to a radiator.

"Why can't you let me go home at night after work? Why do I have to stay here? If the money's good enough, I'll do anything."

"Earlier you said no kinky shit."

"Yeah, well, I didn't mean it."

"To answer your question, I don't trust any of you lot not to tell certain people about what I expect you to do. My mum taught me never to trust anyone except myself."

"What kind of thing am I going to be doing? You mentioned a ritual. What's that about?"

"Fantasy will tell you later. First I want to discuss you and your family and whether anyone's going to miss you. Those other three we took were liabilities and had to be got rid of. Too many people were out there looking for them. If you've got nosy friends and family, tell me now so I can end this before I waste any more time."

Vee was going to tell him the truth. "I don't speak to my parents, I've got no friends or siblings, and my last boyfriend walked out on me a year ago. No one would give a shit that I've gone missing."

Apart from my colleagues.

But it wasn't like she could tell them she had any, and she wasn't missing anyway, they knew damn well she'd been taken.

She stared at him through slitted eyes and sipped the new cup of tea.

Mocha watched her, likely waiting for it to land on his face.

Vee smiled internally. She'd unnerved him. Good.

Chapter Nine

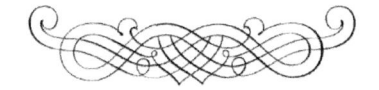

Gideon Mainwaring had had a gutful of people bleating in his earhole at his morning meeting. None of them cared that he'd given up his Sunday for their benefit. He usually had one-to-one chats with individuals but today had decided to have an open house, a free-for-all as it were—and by *God*, he wished he hadn't.

Sometimes, he cursed himself for having what he thought at the time were bright ideas and they turned into anything but. Who could have predicted that an open and honest discussion, which was how he'd put it to them, would turn into something so crass and common?

He shuddered at the memory of when he'd walked in earlier and seen just how many people had come out of their no doubt 'freezing' homes—he didn't believe every single person he spoke to couldn't afford their electricity bill, they were just trying to get some kind of sympathy from him, or, most likely, a grant that they didn't have to pay back, and he'd lost count of the times he'd been informed they were on the 'verge of starvation'.

They must think he was bloody stupid.

The hall had been filled to bursting, lots of bums on seats, not to mention standing room around the edges, people packed in, the types who made it obvious they didn't have a job to go to. Or, to be more specific about it, there were plenty of jobs they could go to but they chose not to apply for them. After all, it was easier to take Universal Credit than actually graft for a living, and then they had the gall to complain that their benefits didn't pay enough. He'd swear half of the ladies he spoke to, the ones with dirty-faced, snotty-nosed children, were doing cash-in-hand jobs because the majority of them had acrylic nails and hair extensions. They really were the dregs of society, scammers, freeloaders, and in his opinion, they were the reason his corner of London was going to rack and ruin.

The air still smelled of too much cheap perfume mixed with the sweat of the unwashed. Why had he chosen this profession again? Good grief.

He could do with some help. He wasn't one to condemn the leaders and what they did, but he'd contemplated meeting the leader of the Proust Estate and asking her to get aboard his ship and help him make a difference—a real difference, getting these lazy bastards out to work. That wasn't possible, though, at least not out in the open. They'd need private, covert meetings, their allegiance kept a secret. Any work the leader did would have to be behind the scenes. A man like him consorting with a leader in keep-them-a-secret shenanigans would be frowned upon.

As would anyone finding out about the rituals.

Christ, he'd worried that someone in the audience would somehow know about them and announce to everyone there that he was involved. Of course, that wouldn't have happened, they were all sworn to secrecy and threatened with exposure if they dared to open their mouths, but it still didn't stop him from fretting.

He'd never run one of these open-house efforts again. Too anxiety-inducing.

He glanced around as the last few residents shuffled towards the door. Their complete takeover of his meeting had come about because of the proposed housing estate that had been earmarked to be built on land where dog walkers felt it was their God-given right to allow their mutts to shit through the eye of a needle on a daily basis as though the area belonged to them. He had an idea that some of the people had banded together prior to the meeting so they could ambush him. He'd had to explain that the person who'd sold the land to the developer had every right to do so and did not have to consult with members of the public to ask for their permission. The entitlement of some blew his mind, but he was a little bit annoyed with her. She'd swanned off into the sunset with a shedload of money and probably wouldn't look back, leaving Gideon to try and smooth over the ruffles she'd created.

He hated it when other people's actions affected his life, which was a stupid way to feel, considering his job was to have his life affected by other people's issues. He was here to fix them or to at least make a show of giving it a good go—the latter was his preference, where he offered lip service but not many actual solutions.

Today's lot had been a hard sell. He didn't think he'd fobbed them off as well as he usually did. They hadn't been interested in the affordable housing that had been proposed, or that there would be a brand-new parade of shops, a McDonald's and a KFC on the roundabout that would be the entrance to the estate, and a primary school which included a nursery. He'd tried to sweeten things by saying there would be a free bus service for any children who needed to go to the secondary schools in the area—it was a big fat lie and something he'd have to back down on when the time came. No one cared that there would be a lake, the surrounding area geared towards inviting wildlife to come and stay, a utopia in the middle of an urban sprawl. His argument about the butterflies and bees had been drowned out by jeers and shouts.

"Who gives a fucking shit about butterflies when we won't be able to walk our dogs anymore? Where are they meant to crap?"

He'd smiled patiently. "There are plenty of paid fields in the vicinity for you to make use of."

"We can't afford to pay for the fucking fields! We want to use that one. A tenner an hour is a joke."

"How about the verges alongside the paths?" he'd suggested. "So long as you pick up your dog's mess, then it's permissible for them to defecate there."

"Defecate? What's that mean?"

"Shit," someone had muttered.

Gideon had rather thought that if they couldn't afford to pay for an hour's use of the fields then they shouldn't be having a bloody dog in the first place, but he'd had to sound sympathetic, telling them he'd look into other public areas that allowed dog walking for free. He'd pop it up on the Facebook page.

The last two people left the hall, old ladies who'd been particularly vociferous, *and* they'd eaten more than their fair share of the biscuits he'd provided to go along with the tea and coffee. He sighed with relief, snapped his briefcase closed, his mind already on the Costa latte he'd collect on the way to his lunch appointment with his wife. He needed the caffeine in order to stay awake while he listened to her drivel.

After dealing with the wife, I might well go and see Charmaine.

Another of his little secrets.

He left via the rear of the building, getting into his Lexus and tipping his head back to rest it while he closed his eyes for a moment and transitioned from his work life to his personal one.

He must have drifted off, because the next thing he knew, his phone alarm was going off, the one he'd set to remind him to meet his wife. He had ten minutes to get there, so no time to stop for coffee, for Pete's sake. A quick look at his face in the rearview mirror, a scrunch of knuckles in his eyes to clear away the sleepy dust, and he was on his way.

Three minutes into the journey, a black cab kept drawing close to his rear bumper, the two men inside it either hippies with their long hair, or they were heavy metal fans who had bad eyesight and preferred to wear ugly glasses rather than the contacts Gideon preferred for himself. He didn't fancy an interaction with either type, so he sped up in case his safe style of driving and staying within the speed limit was getting on their nerves.

He turned left.

They turned left.

God, had they been in the audience at the meeting and he hadn't noticed? Had they decided to follow him, either to shit him up or to shout at him when he finally got out at his destination? They might even throw eggs at him. Or overripe tomatoes.

He joined an A road, one he'd only need to be on for two minutes, then he'd meet his wife in the pub on the roundabout at the top of the off-ramp, one that stood beside a Premier Inn. The taxi still followed, but it had moved to beside him, the passenger staring across and gesturing, his expression one of concern. It seemed the man wasn't menacing at all but trying to get him to stop, keep pointing towards the back of the Lexus.

Gideon indicated to get off on the nearest lay-by, shielded from the road by a thick row of trees.

Perhaps he'd made a mistake there, but it was too late now. The taxi drew up in front of his car, the passenger getting out. Perturbed, Gideon remained in his vehicle—he wasn't stupid enough to get out, although he now felt stupid for stopping at all—and let the window down a short way.

The passenger came to talk to him. "Your brake light is out on the left-hand side, mate, and there was a copper back there, so he might have clocked it."

"Oh, thank you so much for telling me."

"Hey, you're the councillor, aren't you? Gideon Mainwaring?"

"That depends on who's asking." Gideon let out a stupid little laugh. God, he could punch himself in the face sometimes with how ridiculous he behaved.

"As you're now on the outskirts of the Cardigan Estate and not the Proust, the person who's asking is George Wilkes." He produced a gun and poked the business end through the gap in the window. "Let's have a nice little chat, shall we?"

Chapter Ten

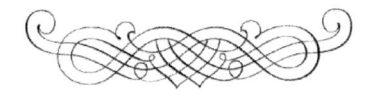

George left Gideon Mainwaring tied up in the boot of his Lexus where he'd been interrogated then had his throat slashed. The useless bastard hadn't wanted to tell him anything at first, babbling on about it all being confidential, but he'd soon given up the name of the Cricketer's Arms. There was a definite link there, it was just a shame the real name of the real bastard behind this gig hadn't been disclosed.

George thought about what Jerry had said, where so long as you had enough money you could become involved in something where posh people played a part, even if you didn't belong to the same circle yourself. And he thought about the pub in question, how it catered to the working class. Mainwaring would have stood out as not belonging, but then maybe he'd drunk there as a way to make it look like he *was* one of the masses, wanting the same as the residents, even though it was completely clear that he wasn't and didn't.

Fucking toff prick.

Mainwaring had said he'd gone to the Cricketer's to drop the money off before each Saturday night, the only way he felt safe enough to hand it over, leaving it in the men's loos. That didn't match what Jerry had to do, though—*if* Jerry had told the truth about handing five grand over out the back of the pub.

George got in the driver's seat of the Lexus and followed Greg on a convoluted route all around the houses until they were away from cameras. Then they went to the warehouse. He'd leave the body in the cellar, have a quick shower and a change of clothes, get Dwayne to collect the Lexus, then go and see the other fucker. The MP. Maybe that bellend would give them the information they needed. And if he didn't? What was another dead body to add to the tall pile that George had murdered during his lifetime?

Chapter Eleven

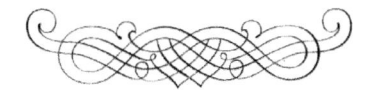

Mocha had trusted Fantasy to deal with Vee, dishing out the instruction that she was to be taken upstairs to the 'dormitory' and introduced to the other women. Tara had been so good at describing the inside of the house that Vee could have made her way up to that room all by herself, but she walked up the

wide staircase beside Fantasy as if she didn't have a clue where she was going.

There weren't any other cameras that she could see.

"Why are there only cameras in the kitchen?"

Fantasy checked behind them, maybe to see if they were being followed. "Because of the knives. If we're cooking and Mocha and Julian aren't in the kitchen with us, one of them will still be watching."

"Right."

Instead of going to the end of the landing and entering the room there, Fantasy gripped Vee's wrist and tugged her into a small toilet with a sink and a slender laundry basket with a lid. She shut the door and leaned on it, staring at the ceiling as if to calm any racing thoughts. Vee watched her carefully and lowered herself onto the closed toilet seat, waiting for what she had to say.

Fantasy dipped her head to look at her. "I felt the phone."

"I know. Why didn't you say anything to them? I thought you were well under Mocha's thumb, even Tara said so." Vee had let that snippet out deliberately.

"Tara? Fucking hell, we were told she'd died."

"She didn't."

"Who the fuck *are* you?"

Vee judged the woman—she felt she could trust her. "She made it to the police station and spoke to me."

"Is she okay?"

"She's in therapy now, but yes, I think she's going to be all right."

Fantasy seem to twig that something Vee had said wasn't quite right. "Hang on a second. You said she made it to the police station and spoke to you*... Are you...?"*

"I'm a copper, yes."

"Oh, thank God. I'd begun to think we'd never get help."

"Unfortunately, Tara didn't see the outside of this house in the daylight so has no clue where it is, and the plan was for my colleagues to follow us tonight, but that's gone to shit. She mentioned others had been taken from the industrial estate. She couldn't tell me the location of the stones either—she said they're fake. The stones, I mean. Is that true?"

Fantasy nodded. "They're stored in the barn out the back and taken to various locations around here in a big lorry. They're made of fibreglass and have weights in the bottom. I'll tell you about the rituals when we're with the other women—I'm almost certain one of them is a snitch, so if we don't chat about it she's going to let Mocha and Julian know. Don't you dare tell her you have a phone or that you're a copper or that you know Tara. Don't tell either of them."

"Why don't any of you ever run away when you're out in the open by the stones?"

"Like I said, I'll tell you when we're with the other girls. We'd better go. They know I went out with Mocha to go scouting tonight so they'll be expecting us. If I were you…just act vulnerable and frightened for the first few days."

"Which woman do I need to worry about?"

"She calls herself Pearl."

"Okay."

Fantasy pushed off the door and opened it, moving round to peer out onto the landing, then gesturing for Vee to follow her. They walked to the door at the end, and although Tara had told Vee about the other women here, she hadn't mentioned Fantasy or Pearl, so they must definitely have been taken after Tara had escaped months ago. Where from, though, if they weren't the three women abducted by the industrial estate? And what went on, did each batch of women pass on stories about others? Had Mocha let them know Tara had existed at some point?

I'll soon find out, providing they even want to talk to me.

Fantasy entered the room first. So the two ladies inside had been allowed to roam the house freely while the others were out? Did they never try to escape?

"This is…" Fantasy turned to Vee. "You can tell us your real name if you want, but Mocha prefers us to have a working name."

A brunette lounging on a double bed sat up and stared over. She had Pearl studs in her eyebrows and nose. No need to guess what her name was, then. "You look like a bit of a princess to me."

Funny, because Vee had chosen something similar. Regal. "Empress."

"What happened?" *the other brown-haired woman asked.* "I'm Candy by the way."

"And I'm Pearl." *It seemed this one didn't like to be left out or have any attention on someone else.*

She was going to get on Vee's nerves.

"Let her get her breath back for a minute," *Fantasy said*. "Then she can tell you."

"Are you from the same place as the others?" *Candy asked*. "Only, I think that's a bit dangerous going there, considering they've been abducted then murdered."

"Murdered?" *Vee stared around at them as if she had no idea what had been going on*. "What the bloody hell's been happening here?"

"Tell us about you first." Pearl got off her bed and came over, taking Vee's hand and guiding her to another bed between hers and Candy's. "Get comfortable. Fantasy will get you a drink."

Vee sat on the bed against the headboard. Fantasy walked to the end of the room where a kitchenette stood against the wall beside a door Tara had said led to an en suite. Fantasy put the kettle on, and it amazed Vee that these women just seemed to accept their lot. Had their lives been so bad prior to coming here that this was preferable to worrying about where their next meal was coming from? With no bills to pay, and a dormitory to live in, wasn't it better than freezing your tits off out on the street?

Or weren't this lot sex workers?

These were questions she could ask Fantasy when they were alone again, but for now, she'd tell them about herself. She stuck to the truth for the most part, leaving out the bit that she was a police officer. To them she must appear a right saddo: no family (even though it was by choice), no friends (because depression prevented her from having any—or was that herself?), no boyfriend (she had no say in that because he'd walked out on her), and a shitty job as a sex worker that had landed her here.

"Mocha will be pleased," Pearl said. "I'll let him know. It sounds like there's no one to give a shit that you're gone, which means you'll probably get to stay alive like us."

Candy nodded. "He made a big mistake with the other three. Their families went mental trying to find out where they'd gone. I saw it on the news and everything before he nabbed me. Then I got brought here so haven't been able to find out what else has gone on."

"Didn't you ever hope the police would find out where they'd been taken and come and save you?" Vee asked.

Fantasy nodded. "There's always hope, even though Mocha said it's pointless. But yeah, I thought with CCTV and everything, but Mocha said he was too careful."

Fantasy brought the cups of tea over and handed them out. "Stop it with the gossiping for now. We need to get you up to scratch regarding the rituals, then we'll talk about how you have to behave here."

Vee knew what to expect because of Tara's statement, but she listened politely and expressed the appropriate noises in the appropriate places. She doubted anything would prepare her for a ritual in real life, but she'd have to get through it in order to pick up as much information about Mocha and Julian, plus any other men involved, as she could.

"The rituals are on Saturday nights," Candy said, "so you haven't had much time to get used to the idea of performing in one. You'll be thrown in at the deep end tomorrow."

Vee forced some tears out. "I had a feeling I shouldn't have gone out to work tonight. There was something in the pit of my stomach that told me not to go, but I ignored it."

"What's the score out there?" Fantasy asked. "I mean…those three women who were taken from the same corner you were on. What's happening now?"

"It's still all over the papers if that's what you mean."

"Why did you even need to ask that?" Pearl stared at Fantasy as though she hated her. "Mocha told us that's what's been going on. Why don't you ever believe him?"

Fantasy glared back. "Um, maybe because he kidnapped me and held me hostage and forced me to play stupid sex games with men on stones? But hey, far be it for me to actually have a brain and not trust someone because of those things… What is it with you anyway? You always seem to stick up for him. What's he done, promised you special privileges if you report back to him on what we've said?"

Pearl blushed despite trying to look like she hadn't done anything wrong. "Don't be daft."

Vee took over to get the conversation away from Pearl being a snitch. It was a bad move on Fantasy's part to have accused her—now Pearl would be on her guard.

"I read the warning online that no sex workers should go to that corner because three women had all gone missing from the same place. After a while, no one went there. I kept away, too, but to be honest, I'd always made more money there so I went tonight anyway. I was the only one, which should've given me a clue. I got picked up, and here I am. Is this a regular thing, the kidnaps? Have there been others?"

Candy twirled hair around her finger. "We've never met them but we've been told about them. Kind of like 'the women who were here before' stories. There were the three in the news. They were killed. There was another woman here with them called Tara, but she ran away. I can't remember the names of the ones before that."

"Tara jumped out of a moving car," Pearl corrected her, "and it killed her."

Vee didn't look at Fantasy; she couldn't risk Pearl and Candy noticing any secret glances between them. "God, that's awful."

"It is." Candy fiddled with her quilt cover. "So you can kind of see why we've decided to stay put and behave. I'd rather live here than be dead, and it's like I have a family now."

"I suppose." Vee sipped her drink that had gone warm. She darted her eyes at the door to give the impression she was afraid of Mocha and Julian barging in. "Now I know about the rituals, tell me about the rules. I don't want you getting in any trouble for not letting me know."

She settled in to memorise them, reminding herself she was Empress.

For now, her life as Vee was over.

Chapter Twelve

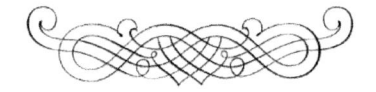

Oliver Prendergast took a deep, calming breath. He looked forward to going home tonight, shutting the curtains, and locking the world away. He worked so hard that sometimes he forgot self-care, and two people today had reminded him that *he* mattered just as much as the constituents. Plus, working on a Sunday and expecting his secretary to do the same? It really had to stop.

Three stories up, he sat at his desk in the window of his office. It overlooked a paved public area with bushes, benches, and trees with such slender trunks they reminded him of Twiglets. A couple rushed from the café opposite towards town, while others seemed in no rush at all, despite the rain pelting down. He imagined many felt despondent; they were already wet, so what was the point in running or using an umbrella? Such a lot of the people he spoke to around here had that attitude, and who could blame them? Their lives were one constant downpour with no chance of getting dry anytime soon. He felt for the lot of them, especially the ones who were *really* trying to get themselves out of the quagmire.

How did you fix a sinking boat if you couldn't afford the tools?

From the alley beside the café, two men stomped towards his building, their black donkey jackets buttoned up to the collars, long hair drenched and lying limp across their shoulders, one blond, the other ginger. Both had their hands in their pockets, and one of them glanced up and caught him observing. Oliver raised his hand—it didn't hurt to be polite—then put his head down to get on with the task at hand: nosing at what a Tory colleague had buggered up this morning.

He'd heard the meeting hadn't gone down too well over on the Proust Estate, and to be honest, Oliver wasn't surprised. He'd warned Gideon that the people there wouldn't take the news of the proposed housing estate lying down, but he'd insisted on taking them all on, trying to persuade them, charm them. Oliver had expected a phone call from the man himself by now; he'd asked his secretary, Jessica, to field any calls from him, saying he was too busy. Listening to Gideon's revoltingly whiny voice wasn't on his to-do list today.

A tap at the door had him lifting his head. "Yes?"

Jessica popped her head round. "Two gentlemen are *insisting* they see you."

"Do they have an appointment?"

"Um, no, but they won't..." She lowered her voice. "They won't go away."

"I see. What is it regarding?"

"They need sandbags for Courtier's Park. It's flooded again because of the rain. They're worried about kids going there."

"Tell them I'll order some bags now to be delivered."

Jessica disappeared and closed the door. Oliver did a search on his computer to find the phone number of a local merchant who sold sandbags—he was a man who stuck to his word, and he'd told Jessica he'd place an order, so he would. Ah, Korr Builders' Merchant, that sounded about right.

Another knock.

"Yes?"

Once again, Jessica's head poked round, and she whispered, "I told them what you said, but they still won't go away. They're insisting that they see you in person." She pulled a face that told him she wasn't happy about having to deal with this by herself.

Not wanting her to be uncomfortable, he stood and said, "Show them in. Thank you." He moved round his desk so he could greet them when they entered. It didn't matter to him who came for a chat, he wasn't the sort who'd be rude and not shake their hand. Unlike Gideon, who was partial to turning his nose up at a bit of honest, hard-work dirt under the fingernails.

The two long-haired men from outside came in.

"Oh, hello, would you like a towel?" Oliver asked.

"We wouldn't mind, cheers," Ginger said.

"I'll ask Jessica to get you a couple straight away."

Oliver called out to her through the still-open door, and she went off to collect them from the bathroom cupboard. Oliver had a shower room here for when he worked late and ended up sleeping over on a pullout chair bed.

He shook each man's hand in turn.

Jessica appeared with the towels, passing them over. "Would you like some coffee?"

She looked at the visitors as though they were the scariest people on the planet, which was unlike her; she was usually like Oliver in that she accepted all walks of life no matter who she dealt with.

"Ta," the blond said, drying his hair.

Jessica went off and closed the door.

"Please, take a seat." Oliver gestured to his computer screen. "I was just about to order the sandbags."

"It's fine, we can afford to pay for them."

Oliver frowned. "I'm sure my secretary said that's what you were here for, that's what you needed."

The men sat on the leather sofa, although had they'd been polite enough to place the towels down first so it didn't get damaged from the wet.

"That was a lie so we could get in to speak to you," Ginger said. "Now then, I've heard you're a really fair fella, the type of man who's going to want to tell us what we need to know."

A sliver of unease went through Oliver. "That sounds a little threatening…"

"It doesn't need to be. If we can just wait for Jessica to bring the coffees, then we can begin."

The door tapped again, testing Oliver's patience that was fraying at the edges. Tell a lie, he was more nervous than impatient. "Yes?"

Jessica came in with a tray of coffee and placed it on his desk. She glanced at the visitors on the sofa then scuttled out. Oliver watched, bemused and curious, and perhaps a tad afraid. He passed the cups over and held out the sweetener. Both of them accepted it, then took the spoons he offered.

"Despite us getting wind of you being involved in a certain enterprise, shall we call it, because of your high standing and the respect afforded to you by other residents, I'm going to do you a solid and tell you who we are and exactly why we're here," Ginger said. "In return, you're going to give me two names and as many addresses as you're aware of regarding those names. Once you do that, you'll tell me you won't have anything more to do with that enterprise. And because of the good you do in the community, we're going to let you live."

Who the bloody hell *were* these people?

"Right..." Oliver swallowed tightly. A swamp of dread filled his stomach. "What enterprise is this?"

"The word *ritual* should help jog your memory."

Oliver had been standing all this time, and his legs gave way. He staggered to an armchair kitty-corner to the sofa, his chest expanding with his sharp intake of air. "What... How did you...? Has the High Priest sent you to trick me again?"

"We've heard he does that, but no, he hasn't sent us to do anything. Look, we introduced ourselves to Jessica, so it's only right that we introduce ourselves to you, and then you'll understand why you need to speak to us. My name is George Wilkes, and this is my brother, Greg."

Oliver thought he was going to have a heart attack. His vision blurred, and his body went cold. "Oh God…"

"I tell so many people this, but He won't help you. Listen to me. It really is this simple: you tell us the real names of Mocha and the High Priest, where they live if you know, their phone numbers, and the address of the house where they keep the women who performed in the rituals—women who were forced to do it against their will, I might add."

"I beg your bloody pardon?" Horrified at that last statement, Oliver blinked to clear his sight and stared over at George. "I swear to God, I thought they were actresses or sex workers, I had no idea they didn't want to be there. I was told they got paid half a grand per ritual, per client."

"You were lied to. They get nothing except a roof over their head and food in their bellies."

"That's just awful. Is there some way I can make it up to them? Pay them what I owe?"

George looked at Greg. "See, I told you I had a good feeling about this one, didn't I." He smiled at Oliver. "So, the addresses?"

"I've got nothing on the women's house, nor Mocha's or Julian's—you're aware of Julian, aren't you?"

"Yes."

"But the High Priest is another matter. The only reason I know where he lives is because the first night I had to drop my money off at the Cricketer's Arms, I waited outside in my car afterwards and followed him."

"How did you know it was him? He usually wears a mask."

"He spoke to me in the toilets, told me where to leave the envelope. I was in a cubicle, and he stood outside it with his feet poking under the door. I waited until I saw the same trainers in the pub, and I have to say, I was most surprised that it was a young kid of about twenty. Whenever you think of a high priest you imagine it's a distinguished gentleman of the older variety, don't you, but no, he had bright-white Nike trainers on and a black tracksuit. He looked the nerdy type, the sort who sits in front of a computer all day and hacks for a living."

"Where does he live?"

"I don't know the exact flat, but he went into a block." He gave them the address.

"The cheeky little fucker!" George barked. "We own that block."

"Oh dear," Oliver said.

"Yeah, oh fucking dear. Tell me more about what he looks like."

"I can't tell you about his hair because it was under his hood, but he's clean-shaven and has a ferret face. I checked on the electoral roll to see who lived in those flats, just in case I needed some insurance, you understand, and I'd offer the list of names to you, but there's no point if they're your tenants."

"There is a point. It'll save us looking them up. We've got loads of flats and loads of tenants."

Oliver went to sit at his desk and launched his private email account on his computer. He opened the one he'd sent to himself containing the list of names and beckoned to George who got up and took a photo of the screen.

"It's that little pleb, I bet you," he said to Greg. "Feeny."

Greg's eyebrows rose. "*Really?*"

"Hmm." George sat back down and addressed Oliver. "Has he got something over you? Has he threatened you?"

"Of course he has, and it's obvious what he can do to ruin me. He'd only have to whisper my name to a journalist, tell them what I've been up to, and my good reputation would be ruined."

"How did you even hear about the rituals?"

"I was on an online forum called Sacrifices, and I was contacted by private message." Ashamed of himself now, Oliver told them his story, of how he'd thought of it as a game, an extension of the board game he'd played in his teenage years, where medieval maidens had to escape from brutish men. "I didn't think there was any harm in it, because we don't actually have sex with the women during those rituals, but we did, err, get satisfied. Since they've been stopped, he made an offer of the women coming to my house instead. I declined, I can't risk anyone being in my private life like that."

George took a gulp of his coffee then placed the cup on the desk. It was still half full. He used a phone, presumably to send a message, and then picked his cup up, leaning back to cradle it. "How the fuck does a scrote like that mastermind such a big operation? I mean, the house the women live in must have cost a fortune. We've been told it's big."

"The rituals have been going on for three years," Oliver said. "I suspect if you have enough cash and a buyer who won't bat an eye at you handing it over in a briefcase, then you can buy a house or whatever the hell you like."

"Yeah, Feeny's on benefits, the council pay us his rent, so on paper it looks like he couldn't afford a house like that. Makes me wonder why he lives in a one-bedroom flat when he could be living in a swanky gaff."

"Maybe the women wouldn't take him seriously if they could see what he looks like," Greg said. "Because I'm struggling to accept it's him."

"What will you do?" Oliver asked.

"There'll be no more threats from him hanging over your head, put it that way."

George went on to tell him about three women who'd been abducted. Oliver recalled it from the news, and his heart sank when it became clear they'd been killed for being too hot to handle. A different one had got away by throwing herself out of a moving car, and another had run from one of the houses just last night. There were three women left, one of them an undercover police officer. That bit of information churned Oliver's stomach, and he selfishly wanted to ask if his name would be brought up to her by the twins and appear in her final report, but he felt it best to keep his mouth shut, considering George had told him earlier that he could walk free from this if he just gave up the information they wanted.

"I won't be getting involved in anything like this again, I can assure you," Oliver said. "And *please* let me give you some money for the women."

"We'll be compensating them for their ordeal, so you can make a donation to a local women's charity instead. I suggest Dolly's Haven."

Oliver nodded. "It's the least I can do."

"We don't want anyone knowing we're involved in this, got it?"

Oh, thank God, they wouldn't be telling the police lady. "Of course."

The twins finished their coffee and stood.

"You've been a massive help, so thanks for that," George said. "Be aware that if we need you in the future, for things going on in the community, then we *will* be paying you a visit and you *will* help us."

Oliver understood. A threat but a mild one. He could cope with that.

Chapter Thirteen

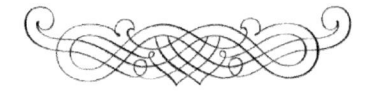

The journey in the back of the lorry with the stones wasn't something Empress had anticipated — she'd thought they'd travel in the SUV, and much later on in the evening, **after** *the stones had been erected. Being squashed amongst the fibreglass monoliths hadn't been on her to-do list. Add a blindfold to that, which she thought was pointless, seeing as they were*

inside a lorry with no windows, and she was completely disorientated. Pearl had warned her not to take the blindfold off because Julian had told them there were cameras. Whether there were or not was a different story. Empress imagined the cameras in the downstairs kitchen were enough of a threat to make them believe he'd told the truth.

Wherever they were going, it took some time to get there, but it could still be in London, probably on the outskirts. It was difficult to gauge the distance travelled—it seemed much longer when she couldn't see. Pearl entertained them by singing for a while, then Candy told some crap jokes. Fantasy remained as silent as Empress.

Finally, the lorry lurched to a stop, and despite knowing what would happen next, she still tensed. Waited. Held her breath.

The sound of the door opening echoed, then a draught snuck in.

"You can take your blindfolds off now and hang them on the hook."

Empress followed the other women's lead, placing her blindfold on a brass hook attached to the interior side of the lorry. Julian stood on the ground, holding out a hand up to help each of them jump down. Empress went last, and even though it was dark, she was going to give it a bloody good go in working out where they were. Yes, the stone locations were different each time, but still.

Ahead, city lights in the far distance. It gave nothing away and resembled any other night-time scene. She walked with the others down the side of the lorry towards some trees—a forest? Were they in Daffodil Woods? No, they couldn't be, the city lights were too far away.

"Wait there," Julian said.

Two men emerged from behind a tree, the size and type of bruiser to punch first and ask questions later. Pearl and Candy chatted to them as though they were old friends, but Fantasy jerked her head at Empress for her to move along a bit, maybe so they could talk in private.

"Who are they?" Empress whispered.

"Bodyguards. A couple more will have already gone to the back of the lorry to help Julian and Mocha with the stones."

At the clatter of what might be a tailgate being lowered, Empress glanced that way. "Oh, there's a ramp, yet Julian made us jump out. Why? And how the hell do they get the stones out of the lorry when there are weights in them?"

Fantasy shrugged. "The same way people deliver heavy furniture. It always sounds to me like there's some kind of mechanical winch whenever they're unloaded."

The rattle of something kept Empress' attention pinned to the lorry. Two men manoeuvred a cage on wheels containing a tall stone inside it. One pushed and the other pulled it down the track and into the forest.

"This is the boring bit," Fantasy said, "where they set all the stones up."

"How long does it take?"

"Depends how far into the woods they're going."

"It makes you wonder whether anyone's tried to run in this kind of situation," Empress whispered. "I mean, should I do it because I'm new and that's what a new person would do?"

"Don't bother. The bloke talking to Candy always carries a gun."

"You didn't tell me that last night."

"There will be loads of things I didn't tell you that will come out. We can't remember everything."

And maybe they don't *want* to remember everything. It's got to be horrible being them.

And it would be horrible to be her, too, because she was one of them now.

She glanced at the man in question and clocked the telltale bulge beneath his jacket. She should have noticed it before, should have given the pair of them a visual sweep from head to toe, but then maybe her instincts had prevented her from doing that because it would have looked too obvious. But would it? A woman new to this game would undoubtedly be curious, but maybe it was better that she hadn't stared at them; she hadn't brought attention to herself.

Pearl gestured for Empress and Fantasy to go over there. She seemed excited, like this part of her Saturday night was the best bit. Did she kid herself they were socialising? Okay, they were, kind of, but Christ, if yakking to heavies was the highlight of the week, then Empress dreaded to think what the other days were like. No one had told her living at the house was bad or scary, especially after you accepted this was your life now and agreed to just get on with it. Mocha was only nasty to get his point across, according to Pearl.

They chatted with the men for a while about news on the 'outside', Candy so obviously eager to hear what the latest trends were on social media that her proclamation that she liked living in the house, living this captive life, might just be a lie if she missed things from her former world. Empress was surprised the men were allowed to tell them anything, but she supposed they'd been given their own set of rules and knew not to cross the line.

This whole setup was fucking weird and mind-boggling. If she didn't know better, she'd say these women were also police officers undercover, because come on, none of them had tried to run, and okay, that bloke had a gun, but surely the natural instinct would be to get away whether your chances were slim or not. She needed to speak to Fantasy out of anyone else's earshot at some point so she could see whether Candy was for real and that she genuinely wanted to stay. If she did, she might become a problem later down the line. How could they rescue someone who didn't want to be rescued?

The last stone in a cage went by, and Empress guessed an hour had passed. Her feet already ached in the high heels she'd been given, and her floaty white nightdress wasn't exactly keeping out the chill. The others had cerise pink ones on. Was hers white to signify purity, to let the red disciples know she was new to this game?

The thought of them coming anywhere near her brought on a shiver.

Mocha appeared from the forest and beckoned them to go with him. He carried a holdall. Candy and Pearl went first, seeming oddly excited to get into the ritual,

Fantasy and Empress following, the burly men behind them. Mocha led them down a track and along a path that had clearly been made by the cages as they'd rolled through the undergrowth.

The lack of foresight here pissed Empress off—they weren't appropriately dressed; her ankle kept turning on the uneven ground because these stupid fucking heels were too high; they'd stood around waiting for perverts to arrive when they could have been sitting in the back of the lorry, at least a little bit warmer... Mocha obviously didn't give a shit about their wellbeing, when he should, considering they made the High Priest a lot of money.

They came out into a small clearing, stones erected on the outside in a circle, four of the 'bed' stones in the middle. Wooden poles had been placed in the ground in between each standing stone, metal bowls on the top with flames stretching out of them. She hadn't seen those being taken out of the lorry and cursed herself for not being as observant as she should have. The whole scene looked like something out of a film—Tara's description was nothing like the real thing.

Her stomach lurched, knowing what happened on those 'beds', and even though Tara and the others had said no penetration was involved, it was still a sexual ritual, one she would have to endure in order to fit in.

She wasn't looking forward to it, but what else could she do but participate? Run? God, no.

Where was Julian? Empress glanced around but couldn't see him. Mocha stood at the clearing entrance with the two big men; the others who'd carted the stones here were nowhere to be seen. Come to think of it, she hadn't spotted any vehicles that these people would have arrived in. Maybe they'd been parked on the other side of the lorry. As a police officer, she didn't like being in a location and not picking up all the facts, even though she hadn't been in a position to do so.

"On the beds," Mocha called out.

Empress felt sick, but she followed the others to the centre of the circle, crying so she looked authentically scared. One by one, they lay on the beds, Empress finding hers surprisingly comfortable—it had a moulded shape that fitted around her body. It was cold, though, and a slight breeze wafted the material of her nightie, lifting it to expose an ankle and shin. She wanted to reach down and cover herself, but the rules were that she folded her arms over her chest in a cross so her fingertips touched her shoulders.

They had to play dead, as if they'd already been sacrificed by the time the disciples arrived. The thought that these people got off on ejaculating over 'deceased' women was revolting.

She stared into the circle of sky visible, stars dotting the darkness, Venus glistening the brightest. Of all the situations she'd imagined herself in, this wasn't one of them. Yes, she'd suggested going undercover, but she hadn't let her mind go as far as putting her into this scene so she could imagine what it felt like. She wished she had, because then she'd have had some kind of warning as to how scary it would be. When Tara had told her, she'd promptly shoved it out of her mind so she hadn't had to think about it again.

The music started. Strange, lilting notes floated around, ghostly and ethereal. Goosebumps rose on her arms and scalp, then she shut her eyes tight, not to block out her surroundings but to make out she was. She had to remember to act like an abductee being forced into this ritual rather than a detective who wanted to find out as much as she could.

She let out a soft sob.

"Shut up," Mocha said. "Get a fucking grip. When the High Priest arrives, I want none of that bloody crying."

She opened her eyes and stared at the sky again, checking her peripheral both sides for when the High Priest emerged. Movement in the trees caught her attention, but she wasn't allowed to tilt her head to see who was coming—one of those bastard rules.

Fuck this, she was going to risk getting a slap or worse. She needed to see what was going on. Crying loudly, sounding more distraught than she felt, she sat up, drawing her knees towards her so she could hug them.

"What the bloody hell are you doing?" Mocha hissed.

She stared across between two thick tree trunks. Someone in a hooded black cloak appeared, followed by others in red. Each of them carried a flaming torch, although the fire looked as fake as the stones. They reminded her of battery-operated candles. She released another sob.

"Shut up," Mocha barked at her, "and lie down!"

She looked over at him and the two men. All of them now had black cloaks on and held fake torches. Empress lowered herself to the stone but turned her head slightly towards the newcomers with their shadowed faces.

No, their masked *faces.*

She whipped her attention back to Mocha and the men. Their faces were now covered in featureless masks made of white plastic. She panicked—it was as if she was outside herself in this moment, she wasn't Vee and she wasn't Empress, she was just a human being experiencing a frightening event. It took a lot of *willpower for her to press down any fear and pull out her courage, at the same time acting like a kidnapped woman.*

"Please, please let me go home," she wailed, hoping she hadn't gone that little bit too far.

Mocha ignored her, thank God. "All hail the High Priest and his red disciples."

This was it now, she was going to have to behave herself, because several other people in black cloaks came and stood around the edge of the circle, the stones behind them, so close to one another that there was no way any of the women could escape if they chose to run. Tara had said each man here paid a thousand pounds—that was a hell of a lot of money. There must be thirty people here.

The music continued to float around, the tempo somewhat faster, though still slow by anyone's standards. The masked High Priest seemed to float across the grass to stand at the base of the four beds, closest to Candy and Pearl in the middle.

He held up his torch and said, "May the sacrifices please our gods tonight."

Then he recited some mumbo-jumbo, could be Latin, could be a made-up language, everyone else joining in apart from the women. Their chanting seemed relentless. It struck Empress then: were any of the red disciples female?

The High Priest finished his babbling and retreated to stand at the edge between two black-cloaked people. The red disciples handed off their torches then parted the fronts of their cloaks to reveal their naked bodies beneath. All of them were men. Empress couldn't stop herself from looking at their erections. She had the sudden urge to bolt but forced herself to remain lying down.

What the fucking hell was she **doing**, agreeing to go undercover?

Bloody hell!

It was over. The High Priest, the disciples, and the circle of watchers had gone, but the women had to remain on the stones until Mocha told them otherwise. Empress' mind flitted back to what she'd experienced. Two disciples had chosen to focus on her as their visual enjoyment, but thankfully, she'd come out of it unscathed. No one had violated her in any way. Had they been instructed not to treat her the same as the others because it was her first night? Or maybe visibly scared women didn't do it for them—she'd cried *throughout the ritual, and a couple of times she'd wondered if the tears and emotions were real. Whatever, she was just glad this had come to an end. At one point the music had reached such a crescendo that the beat throbbed inside her. She hadn't determined what the music was coming out of, but she guessed there were speakers all around.*

She contemplated making a run for it, but she'd promised herself she'd become Mocha's snitch, or at least get him to trust her, and as she'd misbehaved too much already this evening, she needed to pack it in.

"Up you get, girls." He threw packets of wet wipes at the others.

Empress had a strong stomach, but she had to look away while they cleaned themselves up.

The man with the gun went round switching off all the flames on the posts while his mate kept watch over the women. Empress stood, flicking out her arms to try and release some tension, then drawing her palms over her face to brush away the remainder of tears. Her skin was so cold there; the temperature had gone down during what must have been an hour-long ritual, and she couldn't wait to get into her warm bed.

Was this how Candy felt? Was this the worst she'd endured while being part of this weird little family and the house had become her sanctuary despite it being her prison? God knows what this kind of captivity did to someone's brain. Tara had remained relatively sane considering what she'd been through. Fantasy and Pearl also appeared to still have all their marbles, but Candy, there was a vulnerability about her, an innocence, and it didn't sit right that she should be happy to live this grotesque life.

"*Put the dirty wet wipes in this bag,*" *Mocha said.*

So even the DNA was being disposed of. What Empress couldn't get her head around was how some people could think this…whatever this was…was okay, but then some people would do anything for money, wouldn't they, no matter how immoral it was. With thousands of pounds being paid every Saturday night, the High Priest stood to make quite a sum even with 'wages' being paid out. The stones themselves must have cost a fair bit.

Where had he bought them from? She'd already looked into that when she'd worked the case, speaking to person after person who would have the knowledge of how to make the stones in the first place, or film companies that would own them for scenes in Westerns and whatever, or theme parks needing them for decoration. As far as she'd made out, no one had sold a set of stones, nor had they been commissioned to make them for a private buyer. But not everything had a trail, and not everyone was willing to reveal things to a copper. But as well as one or all of the main players here, someone, somewhere, knew where they'd come from.

This operation would have to be run pretty tightly in order for no word about it to have been leaked. Empress and the team hadn't heard about any weird rituals until Tara had come along. The people who paid to engage in this kind of activity were the type who most certainly wouldn't want their names being bandied about, and she suspected they'd been threatened anyway by the High Priest or Mocha to keep everything here a secret.

Thankful to be back at the house, Empress had a shower and chose one of the sets of new pyjamas still in their packaging inside the wardrobe next to her bed. Her bed. It wasn't *her bloody bed, yet it was.*

She wished she was at home.

She shuddered as the music from the ritual piped up inside her head. She'd never forget it, how creepy it was, how the red disciples had danced to it while touching themselves, how the watchers in the outer circle fumbled about beneath their cloaks.

It was all absolutely foul.

Making out she wasn't bothered that she had an audience—she was supposed to be a sex worker, after all, someone who didn't mind others seeing her body—she dropped her towel and put the pyjamas on, then hung the towel on a radiator and went to the kitchenette to make tea for everyone—they'd been sent to the dormitory after having a Chinese in the kitchen downstairs, the food something she hadn't expected.

Mocha had said it was a treat for them behaving so well, although he'd given her a filthy look, then said, "But you'll do better next time, won't you." An order not a question.

She'd nodded.

Fantasy was currently in the shower. Pearl and Candy sat on one of the beds playing cards, their hair damp, cheeks pink from the warmth of their shower water. While the kettle boiled, Empress marvelled at how normal this scene appeared, that to anyone looking at them, everyone would seem happy and content. Nobody would guess what they'd all been through this evening.

Tea made, Empress handed it out, putting Fantasy's on her bedside table for when she came out of the bathroom. Empress sat on her own bed and waited for one of the other two to say something instead of just staring at her.

"You did ever so well," Candy said. "I was in so much more of a state than you for my first time."

"Err, thanks?"

Pearl chuckled. "I like your sarcasm."

"I didn't know what I was supposed to say in response to that," Empress said. "It's not every day you get told you did ever so well while lying on a fake stone in a forest and there are men playing with their cocks. It was like being on a film set. I kept hoping someone would come and stop it."

"Hope is pointless," Candy said, reciting Mocha's words.

Jesus Christ, the woman must be brainwashed.

"I never want to go through that again," Empress said.

Pearl shook her head sadly. "But you have to if you want to stay alive."

"You need to accept your lot." Candy inspected her nails.

Empress blew on her tea and addressed Candy. "You seem to have settled into this way of life quickly." Too quickly? Was she the snitch?

"It's better than what I had." Candy shrugged. "All that's missing is that I can't go into town or go places, but there are books in the library downstairs, so it's not like I don't get to go anywhere at all, is it?"

Yes, books were a good way to take yourself from one location to another without moving from the spot. Candy could convince herself she was in Istanbul with a rich lover when really she was sitting on her bed in this bloody wretched house. Was the woman a bit simple? It worried Empress that she had mental health issues and Mocha was taking advantage of that.

"Do you want to play cards with us?" Candy asked.

"Thanks for the offer, but I need to decompress then go to sleep."

"Don't forget tomorrow is housework day."

Empress nodded. At least with them being allowed to roam the house while they cleaned it, she might be able to find something to give her a solid lead. Tara had tried and failed to discover any paperwork. Empress would have to contact Taylor, too. She'd hidden her phone under her mattress before they'd gone out tonight and would have to get it out when everyone was asleep so she could use it in the bathroom and then stash it in her knickers.

With a bit of luck, when she switched it on it would ping a mast, and if it didn't, then there was some serious bit of kit in this house somewhere that prevented phones from being detected.

Now why didn't that surprise her?

<hr />

DS LITTLE: IN THE HOUSE—NO IDEA WHERE IT IS, WAS BLINDFOLDED. BEEN THROUGH A RITUAL. THERE WERE ABOUT THIRTY PEOPLE TAKING PART. WHAT THE FUCK HAPPENED WITH THE TAIL?

DI TAYLOR: SO BLOODY SORRY, THE DRIVER MADE SURE WE GOT LOST. ARE YOU IN DANGER?

DS LITTLE: NO. IT'S EXACTLY AS TARA SAID. I'M TO DO AS I'M TOLD AND EVERYTHING WILL BE FINE. TOMORROW IS CLEANING DAY. WILL LOOK FOR EVIDENCE. ARE YOU GETTING ANY INFO FROM THIS PHONE, LIKE WHERE I AM?

DI TAYLOR: NOTHING. BLOODY ODD.

DS LITTLE: BUGGER. GOT TO GO TO SLEEP NOW. SPEAK AS SOON AS I CAN.

DI TAYLOR: STAY SAFE.

Chapter Fourteen

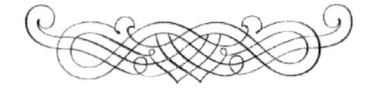

Mr Moody stood at the bar in the Cricketer's Arms and sipped at a pint of non-alcoholic lager. He'd been listening to many conversations since his arrival, and none of them had given him the information he'd been told to watch out for. Surveillance was the type of job where you had to be prepared to stand there for hours, and he'd do that until someone relieved him later on.

After that, he reckoned he'd take his missus out. He earned a hell of a lot more money now he worked for the twins, and his life had changed dramatically. Paying off debts had helped with his mental health, and everything was a lot rosier.

His message tone bleeped, so he took his work burner out of his pocket and accessed WhatsApp. The twins had sent some information to add to what he already knew regarding this 'investigation'.

GG: BY PROCESS OF ELIMINATING THE OTHER TENANTS IN THE SAME BLOCK OF FLATS WHERE HE RENTS FROM US, WE WORKED OUT WHO THE HIGH PRIEST IS. A BLOKE CALLED FEENY. EARLY TWENTIES, SKINNY, FERRET FACE. USUALLY IN BLACK NIKE TRACKSUIT AND WHITE TRAINERS. HE'S ONE OF OUR TENANTS BUT ISN'T AT HOME, SO WE'LL BE ON THE LOOKOUT FOR HIM AS WELL.

Moody wasn't surprised. Young people did all sorts these days, and this one had proved you didn't need to be a sophisticated older man in order to scam thousands of pounds out of perverts. With this Mocha fella in charge of the women along with the other bloke, Julian…they probably acted as the muscle because Feeny was too slender to appear imposing. He hid behind a veil—or a cloak and mask—projecting what he wanted people to see and hear, when all the while he could be mistaken for a weedy little drug dealer.

MOODY: ROGER THAT.

Moody turned to lean his back against the bar. As nonchalantly as possible, he glanced around, starting from the tables to his left. A group of girls he swore were underage sat and joked around. A fair few men obviously having a liquid lunch, probably while their missus cooked a roast at home. A couple of women, babies in buggies, drank coffee and ate muffins. A gentleman sitting on a stool at the bar—he didn't belong here, that much was obvious. He seemed jittery, kept darting his eyes from side to side. Their gazes locked, so Moody gave one of those awkward nods of greeting and added a smile for good measure to let him know he wasn't anyone to worry about.

The door to the street opened, and there he was, the target, exactly how he'd been described, but he had his sweatshirt hood up. He gave the area a quick shufti then headed for a door mark

TOILETS. The jittery man grabbed his pint and necked half of it, then placed a hand on his chest and breathed heavily. Had he come here to drop some money off? If he hadn't, then he needed to get to the doctor sharpish to sort out his nerves.

Moody's objective wasn't to mollycoddle some bloke shitting bricks, so he followed the ferret and found him rooting through a bin in the men's.

"You could catch all sorts doing that," Moody said, right behind him. "Feeny, isn't it?"

The lad spun round, an envelope in hand. "What the fuck's it got to do with you?"

"It's got everything to do with me when I've been told to pick you up." Moody snatched the envelope from him and stuck it in his jacket pocket.

"Oi, that's mine!" Feeny made a grab for it.

Moody clamped a hand around Feeny's wrist and squeezed hard. "What's going to happen is we're going to walk out of these toilets, back through the bar, and you're going to point out whoever put that envelope in the bin so I can give it back to them. Then we're going to leave, get in my stolen car, and—"

Feeny brought his knee up. Just in time, Moody stopped it from making friends with his bollocks by hand-chopping the lad's thigh. Feeny growled in frustration. Still holding his wrist, Moody twisted it behind Feeny's back and manoeuvred him towards the wall. He pressed him to it, the dickhead's cheek squashed against the white tiles.

"You didn't let me finish," Moody said. "And I'm going to drive you to a location that belongs to the twins."

"Shit."

"Yeah, shit," Moody said in his ear. "And all the other swear words you can think of, because you're in a fuck ton of trouble, kid. All I can say is, I'm glad I'm not you."

MOODY: TARGET IS IN BACK OF VEHICLE.

GG: ANY CHANCE YOU CAN HOLD ON TO HIM FOR A BIT? WE CAN'T GET TO DESTINATION YET AS NEED TO PICK SOMEONE ELSE UP.

MOODY: IN LAY-BY BEHIND INDUSTRIAL ESTATE, SO WILL STAY HERE.

GG: NO, POLICE COULD BE PROWLING. PARK BY WAREHOUSE.

MOODY: ON WAY.

Chapter Fifteen

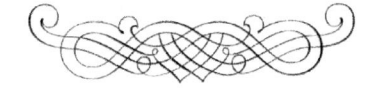

Greg understood George's reasoning regarding keeping Oliver alive but killing Jerry. One was useful to their future, the other wasn't. One could keep a secret, the other was a bigmouth (going by Colin's report on the man and his parties). Although... Fuck it, Greg was going to have to say something.

"Are you sure we ought to leave Oliver alive? Could he become a loose end?"

"I think he's genuinely sorry about the women missing out on the money, and as for him thinking they were sex workers or actresses, I believed him, didn't you? I mean, think about it. If you were that way inclined and you went on a forum that catered to your kind of thing, and you were able to get in touch with a man who could provide it for you, and that man told you he had willing women to participate so long as you had the money, of course you're going to go ahead. You're going to believe what you're told, especially if the bloke's convincing enough. Oliver got caught up in something he thought was a properly arranged event—or events, seeing as they happened every Saturday night—and now he realises he was lied to. He's not going to want anyone to know what he's been up to, his career is too important to him, therefore, he'll keep his mouth shut. Whereas Jerry…"

"Right. So long as you know what you're doing."

"In other words, if this comes back to bite us on the arse later, then it's my fault."

"Yep."

"Whatever."

Greg turned down the track that led to the cottage. "I'm going to have to change out of these clothes. I'm damp, uncomfortable, and this coat smells like wet dog."

"Same."

They still had their disguises on from when they'd been to see Oliver. Greg couldn't wait to get the wig off, not to mention the beard. They could change into clean tracksuits and leave their other stuff to dry on hangers in the kitchen; they'd left the heating on sixteen degrees over the winter so the pipes didn't freeze. With spring just around the corner, they could stop doing that soon.

He parked and got out of the van, going round to the back. From the toolbox, he fished out a couple of cable ties and two microfibre cloths. It'd be better to transport Jerry to the warehouse while he was alive—or, more to the point, it'd be less messy. No blood to clean in the steel room and out of the van, no DNA to worry about.

George had already gone indoors, so Greg joined him in the bedroom. Beard and wig off, clean and dry clothes on, Greg felt a lot more human. In the bathroom, he towel-dried his hair and combed it, washed his face, ignoring his reflection in the mirror above the sink. Sometimes he found it hard to look himself in the eye just before they did bad shit. Only sometimes, though.

He followed his brother into the steel room. Jerry's bloodshot eyes indicated he'd either been crying or had fallen asleep while they were gone. If only the bloke wasn't such a blabbermouth, they could have got away with giving him a major warning, cutting off a few of his fingers to make it clear he *had* to keep things to himself, but honestly, you only had to look at him to know that wasn't going to work. Yes, he'd got away with not telling the police anything this time, but they'd be back to question him, and if they leaned on him hard enough, he'd likely cave under pressure.

He'd tell them the twins had interrogated him.

He had no remorse about the women not getting paid and didn't seem to care that they'd been forced to perform in the rituals. Where were the other women from over the years, the ones before the three in the news? Could they still be alive, or were they dead? At what point had Feeny decided they'd outlived their usefulness?

Or had all of them done something wrong, angering Feeny, who'd then ordered Mocha and Julian to get rid of them?

Before George could ask Jerry any questions, their work burner buzzed with a message. Greg leaned close to so he could read the screen.

COLIN: BEEN 'CASUALLY' TALKING TO THE COPPER INVOLVED IN THE CASE. THE WOMAN WHO THREW HERSELF OUT OF THE CAR, TARA ECCLES, IS IN THERAPY. SUGGEST YOU LEAVE HER ALONE AND COMPENSATE LATER WHEN THE DUST HAS SETTLED. WILL PASTE HER STATEMENT IN AN EMAIL SO YOU HAVE MORE TO GO ON REGARDING FINDING THE MEN.

GG: CHEERS. ALREADY FOUND HP. CHATTING TO HIM SOON.

COLIN: WILL HE DISAPPEAR?

GG: YEAH.

COLIN: GOOD, SAVES ME LIVING ON EDGE, WONDERING WHEN THE BODY WILL TURN UP.

GG: LOL. WE'D HAVE LET YOU KNOW ANYWAY.

COLIN: ALSO, JULIAN'S WIFE AND KIDS WERE MOVED FOR THEIR OWN SAFETY AGES AGO BY THE POLICE.

GG: RIGHTIO.

Greg glanced at George. "Want me to read the email and give you the gist after?"

George nodded. "Yeah, I'll stay with this prick, see if he's willing to talk this time."

"I've told you all I can," Jerry wailed.

Greg left the room, glad to be out of there. Jerry had the air about him that made you want to punch him in the face for no reason. And there were certain people, weren't there, who looked like they needed a bath, even though they appeared clean, as though all the dirty things they'd done lived on their skin and gave them a filthy aura. Greg couldn't describe it any other way—Jerry was a filthy human being in more ways than one, and being in his presence was unsettling and vile.

In the kitchen, Greg opened Colin's email and skim-read the first half of the statement. Tara had described the boarded-up house much the same as Fantasy had, plus the way she'd been treated by Mocha who'd been the bully of the two men. She'd spoken kindly about Julian, although he had, at one time, shouted at her, later apologising because Mocha had forced him to have a go at her, saying he was being too soft.

The night she'd flung herself out of the car, they were on their way to a ritual. Greg wondered if the switch from the SUV to the lorry as a form of transportation had come about because of what Tara had done. At least having the women in the lorry meant they couldn't escape if the doors were locked from the outside.

> *I sat by the car door and judged that we were on the long road we usually travelled for a while just after we'd left the house. For some reason there never was much traffic, not that I heard anyway; could the house be in the middle of nowhere? I couldn't see because we always had to have blindfolds on. I remember I kept wishing a car would come along, or the sound of it, so if I threw myself out, someone would stop and help me. In the end, I couldn't stand the thought of going through yet another ritual any longer and I undid my seat belt, coughing to hide the click. I was shitting myself in case some sort of alarm went off on the dashboard panel to show them I'd taken it off.*

Anyway, it was one of those times where it was now or never, so I felt for the door handle, went through my head how I could quickly throw myself out, pretended it wouldn't hurt, then did it, surprised the child locks weren't on. I landed on my side and rolled onto my stomach. The pain was so bad, but I got on my hands and knees and scrambled onto the verge. I took the blindfold off and checked down the road. The SUV had stopped, and both the front doors opened. Mocha and Julian got out, and the indicator lights flashed to show they'd locked the other women inside.

I ran into the tree line. They shouted at me to stop, but I kept going, right over a field and towards a farmhouse. I looked over my shoulder at one point, to see where the boarded-up house was, but there was nothing standing out to me, so we must have travelled farther than I thought before I'd jumped out. I looked over my other shoulder, and they weren't following me anymore. They'd probably seen where I was going and I knew I'd get there before they could catch up with me, so they were better off getting back in the car.

The farmer let me in to use his phone. His wife was really nice. To get me through the interview, I focused on going home. I didn't think I'd get out of that house alive. I can't believe I'm still breathing.

Greg had the massive urge to go and smack the shit out of Jerry for being a part of this poor girl's story. Saying that, he may never have been at any rituals where she'd been present, but he was still involved in the scheme, he'd still participated in *other* women's stories, so he was guilty regardless.

Greg stormed from the kitchen into the steel room, giving George the phone. He stared at Jerry and asked, "Could you sleep at night knowing what you know now?"

"What do you mean?" Jerry had a new black eye, and blood trickled from one side of his mouth from George 'chatting' to him while Greg wasn't there.

"Let's just pretend we're going to let you go. When you go to bed tonight, will you sleep knowing that those women were forced into those rituals and to go to your house? Will you settle knowing they never got paid a penny? Is your conscience clear enough that you think it's absolutely okay for one of them to have thrown herself out of a car, regardless of whether it would kill her, just so she could get away from the High Priest and Mocha? Can you honestly say that you're fine that those women were scared out of their minds?"

Jerry puffed air out and then winced because it probably hurt his split lip. "George has told me that I've got to tell the truth, so I will. Yeah, I'd probably sleep fine."

Just as Greg thought. This bastard had no empathy. "This one's mine," he told George. "You can have the other two."

"What other two?" Jerry asked, as though he really didn't get it that he was going to be dead soon.

Greg shook his head at him. "Do you know a lad called Kieron Feeny?"

"Nope."

"He lives in the flats down Cromwell Road."

"So?"

Jesus Christ, his arrogance really got on Greg's tits. "What part of 'I'm chained to a ceiling with The Brothers standing in front of me' don't you get?"

"Sorry, sorry, I keep reverting back to being a bolshy bastard. I told you I needed some time away so I could change. Will you let me down so I can get some sleep? I'll stay in the cottage for however long you want me to, you can lock me in if you like, but I'll turn over a new leaf, I swear."

"I don't believe you."

Greg went over to the handle on the wall and turned it to lower the chains. Jerry sighed with relief when his feet touched the floor and yelled loudly as the pressure in his armpits eased. Together, Greg and George took off the manacles, then George moved behind Jerry to wrench his wrists behind his back. Greg snapped the cable ties in place, taking the cloths out of his pocket and stuffing them into the wanker's mouth. Jerry's words were muffled by the material, and at this point, Greg didn't give a single toss what he had to say. It would be pleading, no doubt, which he'd continue at the warehouse when the cloths were removed. That whiny voice of his would get Greg's goat, which wasn't a bad thing on one hand because it'd give him a dose of anger in order to finish him off, but on the other, he didn't want to give this prick the satisfaction of knowing how much he'd affected him.

"Let's go," Greg said.

He wanted to clock Jerry's reaction when he saw Feeny. Had Jerry just lied about knowing him? They'd soon see. Unless Jerry was an expert at hiding his emotions, the truth would be plastered all over his face within the next half an hour.

Chapter Sixteen

Empress had been given the job of cleaning the kitchen, which pissed her off because she'd wanted to go in the office or the library. She'd had a tour of the house this morning, minus the old black laundry room. The library was of particular interest to her as it was a **proper** *library, packed with books, modern paperbacks down one side, old-fashioned leather-bound hardbacks* *on the other. Mocha clearly like to read as he'd been sitting in a wingback chair by the window with a book open on his lap when Julian had shown her inside.*

Julian was in the kitchen with her now, likely told she had to be watched until they could trust her—or, to be truthful about it, until they'd brainwashed or frightened her into wanting to stay. She recalled yesterday's antics of trying to open the back door and failing. How stupid she must have looked, but she'd been more interested in playing her part than worrying about how she'd been viewed.

She sprayed the kitchen cupboard fronts then got on with wiping them over with a microfibre cloth. "Do you like doing this?"

"What, watching someone clean a kitchen?" *He smiled.* "On a serious note, no, I don't like holding women captive, I don't like doing what I do here or at the rituals, but like you, I have no choice."

Was he telling her this because he genuinely needed someone to talk to, or was it something he'd been told to tell her?

"So you were kidnapped off the street, were you?" *She flicked the cloth to get the dust off it.*

"No, but I was visited in my flat and taken out of it."

"Were you brought here?"

"I was."

"Were you blindfolded?"

"No. The threat against my family was enough to keep me from doing anything silly like telling someone this address."

"Family?"

"My wife and two children. Boys."

Christ, now that was something Tara hadn't shared.

"Why are you telling me this?" she asked.

He shrugged. "Maybe I just needed to get it off my chest for once. Maybe you've got one of those faces which makes me want to share the fact that my life is just as shit as yours."

"Does your wife know where you are?"

"No, she probably thinks I left her. She was away with the boys when I was taken from our flat. She'd gone to Southend for the weekend to see her parents. When she got home… Well, let's just say Mocha kept an eye on things for the High Priest. She reported me missing, and I've done my best never to be seen by her or the kids again, although I do stand outside the school at playtimes every now and then."

"How long have you been away from them?"

"Too bloody long."

"And not once have you tried to make contact?"

"Nope. I don't want them shot—and they would be. I've been there when it's happened to someone else. Once the High Priest has got his claws into you, with Mocha acting as his mouthpiece, jailer, whatever you want to call him, there's no getting away alive."

She was about to refute that and say Tara was alive but stopped herself just in time. "The others said that Tara was killed because she fell from a moving car. Was that true?"

She prayed he'd tell her the truth. If she couldn't gain Mocha's trust, then Julian's would do.

"To be honest, we don't know where she is," he said. "She could still be alive for all we know. But you mustn't let on that I told you. By the time we stopped the car and went back to get her, she was off and running."

"You say 'we'…"

"Me and Mocha."

"Does the High Priest know she could still be alive?"

"Fuck, no. We had to tell him she was dead."

"I don't get why you're trusting me with this. I could go back and tell the others—Mocha even—and you'd be right in the shit."

"But you won't, because without me here to look after you all there'd be someone else, and that someone else won't be as nice. Ask the others, I'm gentle and I'm fair. Whatever you may think, I try to treat all the women like I'd want my wife to be treated, with respect and kindness. Granted, I don't always manage it. When Mocha's around I sometimes have to pretend to be more of an arsehole, but like I'm telling you, I also told the others that it's my way of getting through it — of us all getting through it. Behaving ourselves means we stay alive."

"Do the others know you were forced here?"

"No, but I think Fantasy's guessed."

"I feel sorry for you, especially if you've been made to do things you don't want to do. Have you killed anyone?"

"No, that's all Mocha."

"How come you're so sure I won't get away from here and tell someone what you've told me?"

"Because since Tara, we've learned our lesson. This house is like Fort Knox so you can't get out. We always double-check the car doors are locked now once everyone's inside. In Tara's case that was an oversight on Mocha's part."

A noise from somewhere close by had them both staring out into the hallway. Empress' heart thumped far too fast — what if someone had been listening? She held her breath, each thud of her pulse loud, her chest seeming hollow between beats. She stared at Julian, a mutual understanding passing between them: she was going to keep his secret, and he knew it.

With no more noises forthcoming, she picked up the spray and headed into the utility room. She doused the front of the washing machine and tumble dryer, Julian following her to lean on the doorframe.

"I heard there's another laundry room here," she said.

"There is, behind that door there." He nodded to the one beside the washing machine. "Just behave yourself and I'll never have to put you in there. Please, because I really do hate having to be cruel."

She wiped over the appliances and the worktop above them then the cupboards on the wall. She checked inside to find boxes of washing powder and bottles of softener, all so normal. But what had she expected? Tara had told her everything, but when the escapee had first stated she'd been held captive, Empress had imagined a dilapidated building with minimal home comforts, not a house like this.

"Pearl said I need to clean inside the fridge and whatever, but I'll just set the washing machine on a cleaning cycle first."

Empress had memorised the tasks for the kitchen this morning. Once the machine started filling with *water, she took a spray mop out of a cupboard in the utility room and cleaned the floor. Back in the kitchen, Julian swivelling to rest his other arm on the doorframe so he could observe, she got on with emptying the fridge and wiping the shelves.*

Julian told her about his sons, how his heart hurt at the thought of them being upset that he was gone, how he'd never tried to spot his wife since he'd been taken from the flat because if he saw her, he knew he'd call out and then she'd have to die.

Empress put the cheese back in the fridge. "So you keep her image in your head, I suppose."

"I've got a picture of her but don't look at it too often because it's painful."

"This whole thing is such an awful mess."

"What, the fridge?"

She turned to him to see if he was joking. His smile told her he was.

"You have to laugh," he said, "because crying won't get us out of this."

"Neither will doing as we're told. There must be a way we can get word to your wife and kids, make her understand she has to get out of London and get safe, then, because you've got the privilege of being allowed to leave the house and whatever, you could nick the SUV, go and find them. Would she believe you if you

sent her a note that said they had to run? Or would she go to the police? I think what I'm trying to ask is whether she'd take you seriously enough to just do what you said without question."

"She'd phone the police."

"Even if you put something that only you would know—and she'd know only you would know?"

"Believe me, I've thought of so many things I could do, and even though Mocha's an arsehole, he did tell me he wished he had to go and collect someone else, not me, someone without kids, but the High Priest isn't anyone I want to mess with. Mocha won't fuck about with him either, and if they get wind that I've sent a note to my wife, you can imagine what'll happen. I actually think Mocha would get one of you girls to shoot me, then you'd have to bury me out the back behind the barn where those women are."

The barn. Something to tell Taylor.

For months now, Empress had been wondering where they were. There had been hope in the whole team that they had just been taken away, maybe abroad, and they were alive and well. Finding out they were dead was a big blow, so the next step was to unearth the bodies so they could be given a proper burial and the families could get some closure.

The fact that those three women were lying not too far away under the ground made Empress feel sick and so arsey she wanted to punch something.

"What did that ham ever do to you?" Julian asked.

She stared at the packet in her hand where she'd squeezed it. She laughed. "I'm just angry, that's all, how we're being manipulated and there's nothing we can do about it."

She restocked the fridge and moved on to the cooker, getting on her hands and knees and using a wire wool pad to scrub something that was already perfectly clean.

Julian made everyone a cup of tea, and she took a break to drink it with them.

"Where's Mocha?" Empress asked. "Still reading?"

"No," Julian said, "he goes and has a roast with his mum on Sundays."

"Does she know he lives here or does she think it's somewhere else?" Empress asked, trying to be casual about it in case Pearl or Candy were snitches. "Does she visit him here and all of you have to hide?"

"No idea what he tells her," Julian said by way of letting her know he didn't feel comfortable to talk about things now the others were there.

"Do we get to have a roast?" she asked.

He nodded. "You'll all make it while I watch. I have to make sure nobody takes one of the knives. They're counted periodically throughout the prepping session and locked in that drawer there when not in use."

"I take it we'll be having the chickens that are in the fridge." Empress finished her tea and took the cup to the dishwasher. "Shall I start peeling some veg?"

If she pretended hard enough, she could convince herself this was a discussion about dinner with friends who'd all met up together in one of their homes. She used a peeler to take the skin off the potatoes with Julian standing right beside her, and the others went off to finish their cleaning.

He glanced at the door to make sure no one was listening. "Be careful what you say in front of them."

"I gathered that."

"I just don't want them twigging that we've talked. They might tell Mocha." He placed his hand on her forearm. "You won't tell anyone what I've said, will you?"

The pleading and pain in his eyes let her know that he was genuine—or if he wasn't then he was a bloody good actor.

"I won't," she said. "And if anyone asks me what we talked about, because someone's bound to have heard our voices, then we'll just have to say it was about watching telly and stuff like that."

"You'll come to see after a while of living in this house that if you're going to claim you were doing something when you weren't, then Mocha will find out the truth of the matter. We can't just say we were talking about the television, we now have to make sure we both know what particular programmes we were talking about, because believe me, he'll ask questions."

She nodded. "Do you like Coronation Street?"

"Yes."

"Then we'll go with that, but only up until the last episode before I got taken. We don't want to get caught out." She stared at him. "Is this a test? Is this where you tell me you've been playing me this whole time to see if I'd be willing to go against Mocha? Is the story about your wife and kids even true?"

He sighed. "I swear, I'm telling the truth."

"Then why didn't you tell any of the others?"

"Because there's something about you, I've already said that."

"Fair enough." She popped the last potato in a bowl of cold water, handed him the peeler, and got on with putting the scrapings in the bin. She checked the hallway before she asked, "The person who finishes *their room before anyone else gets to clean the library don't they?"*

"Yep…"

"Then someone else can do the carrots and parsnips. I bet you a pound to a penny that inside one of those books is some kind of paperwork. A man like Mocha will have insurance on the High Priest, and I reckon if we look on the upper shelves—or if I look because you'll need to make out you're supervising me—then we can use the scanner and printer in his office to make a copy of our own."

"And do what with it?"

"I don't know, we'll think of something."

He dried the peeler on a tea towel then placed it in the drawer and locked it. "Quickly then, before someone else gets in there first."

She collected a cloth, and they made their way down the hall and into the library. She hadn't noticed it last time she been here, but there was a ladder with wheels which would make her life much easier. She climbed it on the hardback side, going to the top shelf and removing each book one by one, leafing through all the pages and dusting the covers before putting them back. It was going to take longer than she'd thought.

An hour had passed, and Julian called time. "I've got to go and supervise the others in the kitchen while they're making dinner."

Why couldn't he just watch them on his phone?

Or were the kitchen cameras fake?

"Leave me here to get on with this," *she said.*

"That's not normal protocol when someone's new here. They might tell Mocha that I left you alone."

"Then I'll come here when the dinner is in the oven and they're watching telly. What time does Mocha normally get back?"

"About ten."

"That should be plenty of time for me to check each book. If any of them ask me what the hell I'm doing still in the library, I'll say I want to dust all of the books, that cleaning calms me or some bullshit like that."

"Okay, that could work."

They returned to the kitchen, and every one of them pretended to be normal, laughing and joking, telling stories, and once the dinner was cooking, when the others got up to go and watch the telly, Empress announced her mission.

"Rather you than me," *Pearl said,* "because that's one hell of a job. If ever I'm cleaning in there I just flick a duster over the spines, but each to their own."

She swanned off with Candy on her arm, and Fantasy gave Empress a funny look, then glanced at Julian. She made eye contact with Empress again, and it seemed she was asking if she had some kind of plan — to incapacitate Julian maybe? It was a bloody good idea, because he likely had keys to the house, but then did *he? Had Mocha locked them* all *in? Empress shook her head subtly and turned her back on her to walk to the library.*

If she found nothing between the pages of the books, then at least she'd tried. While she was at it, she'd probe a bit more into Julian's role here and whether he did indeed have keys. It could be pivotal to their escape.

If he was even willing to take that risk.

He sat in the chair by the shuttered window while she continued going through the other books. She made it to the bottom row in the hardback section. Kneeling on the floor was hurting her back, so she stretched it out with her hands above her head.

"This could be a lost cause," he said.

"I know, but I won't rest until I've checked them all. Even if we don't find some evidence against the High Priest, because, let's face it, I've probably let my imagination run away with me there, we might find something else. What did he threaten you with other than your wife and kids being killed? What I mean is,

what have you done that he's got such a hold over you?"

"I'd rather not say what I've done."

"Is it really bad?"

"Depends on how you look at it."

"Okay, so if we got out of here and this went to court, would what you did before being brought here impact the length of your sentence?"

"I don't know."

While Empress wasn't going to put all of her eggs in one basket with Julian, he was the closest thing she had to hope, to getting everyone out of here, to having an ally. All right, it could turn out that he was playing her, that she'd been pulled in by the vulnerability he'd displayed, but she didn't think so. She'd spent enough time interviewing criminals and members of the public to know when someone was bullshitting her. Taylor would say you couldn't be sure whether **anyone** was being truthful, but she was at least eighty percent sure Julian was.

That may bite her on the arse later on, but for now, she believed him.

Chapter Seventeen

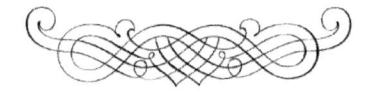

Ever since Moody had punched him in the face outside the Cricketer's Arms, the scrote had slept, the blow knocking him out. Moody had bundled Feeny into the back of the vehicle and returned to the pub, finding the shitting-himself man at the bar. He'd handed the envelope over and whispered, "The deal's off, and if you know what's good for you, you'll never attempt to participate in anything like this again." A little mention of the twins had sealed the deal, and he'd walked out, congratulating himself on a job well done.

That bloke was so frightened that Moody doubted he'd ever breathe a word of what he'd tried to be a part of—who the fuck was interested in sex rituals anyway? Maybe later down the line the man would see it as fate stepping in, doing him a favour, but for now he'd likely have finished his pint and gone home thanking his lucky stars he hadn't lost his money and The Brothers themselves hadn't had a word with him.

After his arrival at the warehouse, Moody had amused himself by playing *Find the Cat* on his phone. He sighed. He had one more cat to find out of forty, and the little bastard wouldn't show himself. Ah, there he was, disguised, stretching up a tree trunk. Level complete, he gave his surroundings the once-over. Movement in the rearview mirror caught his eye. He put his phone away and checked who was coming, prepared to drive off if need be. His number plate was doctored despite the vehicle being stolen, and he could pull his beanie down into its balaclava form if he had to, but there was nothing to worry about.

Calm down.

The twins had arrived in a little white van.

Moody relaxed. They parked up in front of the warehouse. Moody would stay put until he'd had word on what to do next. He'd learned he was allowed to take the initiative when out on jobs alone if he felt it was of benefit, but when George and Greg were in attendance, he was better off waiting for orders. George could be a bit snippy, and Moody had to teach himself to count down from five sometimes before he responded to him; his knee-jerk reaction was to give back as good as he got, but that wasn't wise when it concerned the nuttier twin.

Moody couldn't see what was going on, Greg had parked with the rear of the van pointing towards the warehouse doors, but they were likely taking Jerry inside.

Moody's phone bleeped, and he looked at the message.

GG: BRING YOUR BASTARD IN.

Feeny was a lightweight little cunt, and shoving him over his shoulder would be no problem. Moody got out of the vehicle and collected his quarry, taking him in the warehouse, kicking the door shut and carrying him down the stairs to the cellar.

He found the twins standing beside two guests on the floor. Moody recognised one of them as a dead Gideon Mainwaring, that councillor who was on the news recently. The other he'd never clapped eyes on before, but going by his bruised face and drying blood at one side of his mouth, he'd already been in the wars and was about to die himself.

Rather than ask any questions, Moody placed the still-unconscious Feeny on the floor in the corner, then moved to the bottom of the stairs. "Do you need me to stay for anything?"

George shook his head. "Nah, sort the motor then get yourself off home. Sorry to have got you out to work on a Sunday, but that's the way it is."

Moody nodded and left the warehouse. He'd drive to where he'd left his own car. Dwayne would meet him and collect this one. It would take twenty minutes at the most, then Moody would go home and suggest to the wife that they go out for dinner. She'd been at work herself this morning. He didn't expect she'd fancy cooking, and neither did he.

He drove away, his mind already on filling his belly with a roast, the warehouse and its contents long forgotten.

Chapter Eighteen

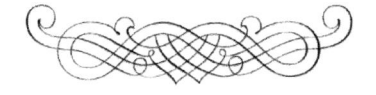

With three targets to deal with, there was a lot to get done. Before the day was over, which was going to turn out to be one of the longest Sundays George had ever lived, he wanted to have found Mocha and Julian. Jerry was a lost cause, so that meant Feeny was the present hope to gather information.

Jerry sat on the flagstone floor beside Gideon's corpse. He whimpered, snot settling on top of a corner of cloth that stuck out of his mouth. He looked a sorry sight, but George had no sympathy for him.

He reached down and took the cloths out. "That fellow there didn't answer all the questions I asked either." He wasn't about to say he'd got bored of interrogating Gideon so had slit his throat quicker than he should have. "And you can see what happened to him, so it won't be too difficult to imagine what's going to happen to you. What I'd *like* you to see, though, is what will happen to you afterwards."

George didn't need to tell Greg what they had to do now. Between them, they undressed the dead Gideon and strung him up above the trapdoor. They covered their clothes in forensic outfits and snapped on gloves, Greg then turning to put on the halogen heater. He sat on a foldout chair beside the tool table, arms crossed, and settled down to watch.

"Please, please," Jerry begged, "I swear to you I won't say a word. I just want to go home."

"It's too late for that," Greg said.

George opened the trapdoor, the sound of the river bursting into the room. He inhaled deeply — that smell was unique to the Thames, it hung in the air and would forever remind him of home. He thought he caught the sound of a distant gull, but it was probably an auditory trick, something his mind had created as he always paired the Thames with those bastard birds that stole your chips.

He plugged in the hedge cutter, approaching Gideon and positioning the blade beside one of his little toes. He glanced across at a wide-eyed Jerry who must have finally realised that shit had got serious; a wet patch stained his jeans, and he choked out sobs.

Again, George had no sympathy.

Switching on the tool, he got to work, pieces of Gideon plopping into the water with every slice, Jerry crying, his eyes scrunched shut. By the time George had reached Gideon's top half, it looked like Jerry was about to pass out through fear that he was witnessing what would happen to him once his throat had been sliced — *if* that's what Greg had in mind for him.

George carved into Gideon's face and head, bits dropping off, then he carved down the middle of the torso, moving to concentrate on the left side and the arm attached. In the end, only hands, wrists, and part of the lower arms remained. Greg took them out of the manacles one at a time and sliced them, leaving the fingers until last. He used cigar cutters on those, and with the councillor's corpse removed from the equation, George smiled down at Jerry.

"Your turn, sunshine."

Jerry shook his head and tried to stand, fumbling the attempt and landing on his side, a skinny beached whale. "No, please, no…"

George wasn't in the mood for fucking about, so he stomped over there and cut off Jerry's thumb to give him something to focus on other than trying to get away. George dropped the cutters in a bowl of bleach water and selected scissors to undo the cable ties. He snipped them to release Jerry's wrists, and Greg stood to help attach him to the manacles. George moved to the wall to wind the chains up, and Jerry rose above the churning water, screaming blue murder, the sound drowned out somewhat by the roar of the Thames.

Greg got to work with the scissors, cutting off the prat's clothes, tossing each strip of fabric to one side. Now they'd had a log burner installed, George fired that up so when it was hot enough and the flames pranced, the clothing would be placed inside. Any ashes would be dumped in the water afterwards.

This place was fucking perfect for hiding evidence.

Jerry cried so much he couldn't breathe properly, and he kept trying to get words out, but nothing emerged except strangled noises that meant fuck all. Greg had finished disrobing him and closed the scissors. He stabbed the blades into Jerry's jugular, a slight smile curving at Jerry staring at him in utter shock. Greg removed the weapon, blood spurting in pulsing arcs. The sound and sight of Jerry trying to catch a breath was a fascinating study, and George imagined it was like being underwater, except Jerry was drowning on blood, his lungs filling with it, the red stuff pooling in his throat, blocking his airway.

Greg picked up the hedge cutter, George surprised that his twin wanted to go the whole hog and cut the fucker up as well as kill him. George took a seat on the chair and watched, transfixed at the sight of someone else doing what he usually did and clearly enjoying it. That was unusual. Greg was the type to get the job done and not derive any sadistic pleasure from it, but it seemed he was getting something out of it this time. Maybe whatever he'd read in that email had pissed him off. George would have to give it a read later and find out.

Ten minutes had passed by the time Greg had finished, and by then Feeny stirred. Probably all the noise. The High Priest didn't open his eyes, though, it seemed he'd gone back to sleep, so George and Greg got the cellar cleaned up a bit using the hose, closing the trapdoor.

In their blood-soaked forensic suits, they stood staring down at Feeny, George looking forward to the fuckwit's reaction when he saw them, his landlords. He kicked Feeny's leg until the kid opened his eyes. They widened, and he scrambled into a sitting position, then shuffled back on his arse to get as far away from them as possible. A bruise coloured his cheek, and it seemed his top tooth had gone through his bottom lip, the type of injury received when someone fell after being punched, the jaw jarred.

Not such a hardman now, was he.

George's mind couldn't marry what he was seeing with what he'd heard about this man—and he used that term loosely. This wasn't a man visually, it was a kid, yet his brain...there was no doubting how clever he was to have pulled everything off. What he'd achieved in such a short space of time was admirable—or it would be in other circumstances.

"What... Fuck..." Feeny's back hit the wall.

"Stand up," George ordered.

Feeny glanced around, his gaze ending up on the floor. Was he calculating that the river was underneath and if he could just get the trapdoor open, he could swim away? For whatever reason, the river directly beneath gushed—maybe there was one of those dams or whatever, George didn't understand how waterways worked, but he didn't rate Feeny's chances if he launched himself into the churning water.

Feeny stood, pressing himself against the wall. He checked the room again. Trying to find Moody? "What...what am I doing here?"

George tutted. "So you're going to play the innocent victim card, are you?"

"I always pay my rent on time, so there's no need for this."

"This is nothing to do with your rent."

"What then?"

"Why do you need to rent off us when you have a big gaff in the countryside?"

The question had caught Feeny off guard, and he paled. "I don't know what you're on about."

"You currently have three women there with Mocha and Julian. The fourth woman ran away last night from a client's house. Jerry. But you know all this, don't you."

"This is nuts. What are you saying, bro?"

"*Don't* call me bro. Now, I think we can dispense with the clueless act, don't you? It's winding me up, and I'm tired, I'm hungry. We've still got shitloads to do, and I just want to get answers out of you and move on."

George had said 'move on' purposely, to give Feeny hope. It lit up his eyes, slanted his mouth into a slight smile.

"What do you need to know?"

"Usually, to string this out, I'd ask what that envelope was for, the one our man saw you take out of the bin in the toilet of the Cricketer's Arms, but I don't want to string this out. I want the address of the house, no fuss."

"What house? You're making no sense."

I'm going to have to torture the fucker.

George sighed and glanced at Greg whose shoulders slumped—he didn't want to have to make a song and dance about this either. A quick nod confirmed his twin would help, so George grabbed one of Feeny's arms, Greg the other. Feeny struggled to get away, but his smaller size meant he had no chance with a man mountain either side of him. George held him by the throat, slightly lifted from the flagstones, so Greg could undress him. Feeny choked, scrabbling at George's gloved hand to try to release the pressure. It wasn't enough to kill the kid or even make him pass out—Feeny was just being dramatic. Panicking, the fanny.

Now stripped bare, he lost some of his fight. Manacles around his wrists, he hung from the chains a foot from the floor, his breathing heavy, sweat breaking out all over him. It glistened from the light of the halogen.

"Please, I don't know what I'm meant to have done wrong."

"Don't give me that bollocks," George said. "You've been the mastermind behind forcing women to do rituals, you've been making them have sex with clients in their homes. You don't pay them a penny. Three of them have been killed—that we know of, or is that a lie? Did you get your buddies to tell the women that so they'd comply quicker? People mistake you for a little dweeb working on his computer, but that's how it all begin, isn't it. You got the idea from somewhere and ran with it. Created a forum online. Where did you keep the girls to begin with, until you'd saved up enough money to buy that house? Or is it rented? That makes more sense, it's less of an initial outlay. That's got to be at least a grand a week, a place that size. And the guns. Where the fuck did they come from?"

"How do you even—"

"How do I even know how big the house is? Because Fantasy told us."

Feeny's cheeks coloured.

George smiled. "People always slip up eventually, and if they don't, if they're really clever and they've got complete control over their tongue, then I usually get bored and kill them before I really should. I'll admit, I *need* you to tell me where that house is, so I won't stop torturing you until you can't take it anymore and you end up telling me. Were you aware you've got an undercover police officer there?"

"You're chatting shit."

"And you're skating very close to a thin line, my old son. The guns. Tell me."

"Fuck off."

"D'you know what, I'm not going to bother talking to you anymore—as in talking to give you a chance to confess, I'm just going to get on with whipping you. My brother will help, and even if it means waiting for you to wake up after you've passed out, time and time again, we'll keep going until you tell us what we need to know."

George turned from him to collect a couple of whips from the table. He handed one to Greg. "You take the top, I'll take the bottom, otherwise we're going to get in a tangle."

Greg nodded and went to stand behind Feeny. "You'd better be mentally prepared for this, kid, because it *really* is going to hurt."

George stood in front of him. "Are you sure you don't want to tell me where that house is?"

"Fuck you."

George grinned. "Fuck you, too."

No part of Feeny's body had been left unmarked. What got George was that all this could have been avoided. There was no need for the split skin, the blood, the eye that had taken the savage tip of Greg's whip when it had snaked round onto his face from behind. The white of the eye was now red, the iris scarlet. Karma had decided to step in and lend a hand, directing George's whip to curl around Feeny's cock and strangle the fuck out of it. If George had tried to make that move it probably wouldn't have worked. He'd tugged to prolong the pain, elongating his dick, laughing at Feeny's screams.

But it hadn't worked, this torture. Feeny had got the guns from someone online. They'd been left in a public bin, everything done anonymously. He hadn't given up the address of the big house, but he *had* given them another. George could only imagine why Feeny had chosen that one to reveal, maybe because the person who lived there had no idea where the boarded-up house was so would be of no use to them, and there wasn't anything they could do now to force Feeny to talk because he'd died unexpectedly. George could only assume he'd had a heart attack or something.

In a rush, George and Greg had taken the kid down and performed CPR—George had been desperate for the information they sought, but the little bastard wouldn't breathe again, and after ten minutes of trying, they'd given up. George had chopped him up, they'd hosed the cellar down again, and he'd fed the clothing and the forensic gear into the fire bit by bit. He'd dispose of the ashes later once the fire had gone out—or he put it out.

Showered and changed into fresh tracksuits, they left the warehouse, George getting a bit hungry, but maybe the person they were about to visit would offer them some biscuits to tide them over. If not, it wouldn't hurt to nip to McDonald's afterwards, just the once. They could eat on the go.

There was still too much to do—providing the person told them what they needed to know. Providing they even knew anything. What was it with people being so secretive lately, having the balls to keep information to themselves? Not for the first time, George wondered if they were losing their touch—or him specifically, seeing as he was the one who did most of the threatening and hurting. Or were people just different these days? More entitled, so when George asked questions, they didn't see why they had to answer if they didn't want to. A few generations had been ruined by the snowflake brigade, in his opinion, parents too afraid to put down rules and expect them to be followed. He'd read an article the other day that said you now had to ask a baby's permission to change their nappy because you were seeing their private parts.

What the actual fuck.

That was what George didn't like. All these stupid rules. Stupid new ways of doing things. And people weren't playing ball, so that meant he didn't feel like he was in control.

It royally pissed him off.

Chapter Nineteen

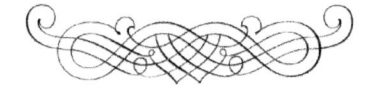

If any useful evidence existed, then it wasn't in the library. There were no hidden panels, no secret shelf doors that she could determine, and she'd even checked down the sides and backs of the chair cushions. Empress had finished the job sooner than she'd expected, and she was showered and in her pyjamas by the time Mocha returned to the house. She sat at the

table in the kitchen with the others around eight o'clock, drinking tea and eating chicken and mayonnaise sandwiches.

He stood in the doorway and stared at them all for a moment, either checking they were all there and no one was missing, or trying to work out whether anyone wasn't to be trusted. Of course his final perusal was of Empress, but she stood her ground and continued eating while maintaining eye contact. Maybe she ought to have been more submissive, but as the newbie, she'd be the first one to be accused of something, so she wanted to let him know she had nothing to hide.

He walked in and plonked himself at the head of the table, leaning back and stretching his legs beneath. He scrubbed a hand over his face. "I've had to come back early."

If anyone in her team had said that, someone would have piped up with a sarky comment like, "Blimey, we'd never have known if you hadn't said," but she didn't think that would be appreciated so kept her mouth shut.

"How come?" Julian frowned. Why, if he was just like the women—a commodity. In his role, did he expect to be appraised of any announcements before Mocha came home, or was he used to hearing information at the same time as everyone else?

"Make me a strong drink because I need it." Mocha gestured to the kitchen area.

Pearl rose. "I'll do it."

Mocha watched her walking away, his sights on her swaying backside. "We've got a problem."

Candy raised a hand to her mouth. "Oh God, has someone reported Empress as missing?"

"I wish that's all it was." Mocha snorted. "One of the red disciples has gone against his word."

Empress didn't know what that meant. "I don't understand…"

Mocha glared at Candy and Fantasy. "I told you to fill her in on everything."

"They did," Empress lied, "but there was so much information that I must have forgotten that bit."

Mocha turned her way. "Disciples promise never to tell anyone about the rituals. One of them, we'll call him Prick-Face, his wife asked why a grand had been withdrawn. Now these men also promise to be careful where their cash comes from and who might notice it going missing. He usually withdraws it from his own account, one she doesn't get to see, but he made a little error, using the joint account instead. She ended up having a go at him, going on and on about the money and how it was supposed to be for a holiday they've been saving for, and he's caved in and told her what he used it on."

"Oh no," Fantasy said.

"She wanted to know the ins and outs, said if he didn't tell her she'd kick him out there and then and he'd never see the kids again, so he told her. I reckon she was hacked off he'd cheated on her. The silly bitch went and phoned the police, didn't she, because she's appalled that 'women are being violated'." Mocha rolled his eyes.

"I don't think we are," Candy said. "It's no different to us working on street corners. Actually, it's less of a risk because we're not actually having sex with anybody."

"Ah, now that's where things are going to change…" Mocha took the drink Pearl handed to him and knocked it back in one. He passed the glass back to her, clearly wanting another.

"What's changing?" she asked.

"The High Priest can't risk doing the rituals now the police have been made aware of them."

They were already aware, and we haven't been able to do sod all about it.

Mocha released a big sigh. "So we're going to begin a new scheme."

"Which is what?" Julian eyed him warily.

"The disciples will pay for you to go to their houses." Mocha flapped his hand at Pearl for her to get a move on with that drink. "Julian, you'll use the SUV to drive partway to the pub on the main road, then you'll get a taxi the rest of the way. Blindfolds are still mandatory."

"Won't that make us more noticeable to a cab driver, though?" Emerald asked.

Mocha stared at her like he wanted to give her a slap. "Look, there's a lot to still be ironed out, and once I know the order of events from the High Priest, then I'll pass them on to you lot. Just be aware that from now on you'll have to service the disciples in a different way because the rituals won't be happening to get them going, and it'll be orgies sometimes so he can still rake a lot of cash in."

"When does this start?" Julian asked.

"As soon as the High Priest tells me it's a go." Mocha stood, downed his new drink from Pearl. "I'm off to bed." He left the kitchen, closing the door behind him.

"What did he mean by servicing them in a different way?" Candy asked.

"Probably actual sex," Fantasy said.

Empress cringed inside. Could she put herself through that for her job? Did she have a choice if she was going to free them all?

"Whatever it is, and I hate to say this, you'll just have to get on with it," Julian said.

"It would be nice if we got paid," Fantasy muttered.

Julian shook his head as if he'd had this conversation with her a million times before. "You know your pay is a roof over your head and food in your belly and being kept safe from nasty punters who'll turn on you."

"I'd only need a little bit, like twenty quid or whatever," Fantasy pushed, "so I can buy some stuff from Amazon. It'd be nice to have the excitement of a package arriving again. I used to love that when I lived in my place."

"I'll ask Mocha if that's something that can be arranged."

"Thanks, Julian, you really are good to us." Fantasy looked pointedly at Empress. "I'm going to bed, too."

Empress stood. "Same."

They walked out of the kitchen and up the stairs. Mocha's bedroom was on the opposite side to the dormitory, but Fantasy still pressed her finger to her lips to warn Empress to stay quiet. They entered the dorm, going into the bathroom and closing the door.

"What was all that about in the library?" Fantasy asked quietly.

"I was looking for hidden papers or some kind of evidence that we could use against Julian or Mocha."

"What good is that to us if we can't do anything with it?"

"Because I'm determined to find a way out of here. Anyway, I have the phone, remember, so I can pass on anything I find. I wanted the address of this place — there has to be something here with that on it."

Fantasy folded her arms. "You seemed to be getting on pretty well with Julian earlier."

"It was our love of Coronation Street that did it."

"Oh God, what a boring time you must have had."

"It was all right. Anyway, I didn't find anything we could use in the library, so if there's something that'll come in handy then it's probably going to be in Mocha's bedroom or the office."

"And those rooms are always locked and no one's allowed to clean them."

"Would Julian have keys?"

"He's got a set for all the locked rooms, plus the house itself and the SUV. He's Mocha's right-hand man, surely you must have noticed that."

"I did, but he doesn't seem the type."

And if he had keys to the SUV, why the hell hadn't he collected his wife and kids and fucked off with them? She was going to have to question him again about that—something wasn't adding up. But unless the car had a tracker on it or Julian was followed everywhere, then who was to know where he went and who he saw? He'd said he'd watched his kids at playtime, so he must be able to get away with no one seeing him.

Empress shoved any deep thoughts about him aside for now. "He might well be a right-hand man, but it was obvious he didn't want to shoot anyone in that car that was following us after I first got picked up."

"Hmm, he's softer than Mocha, and he doesn't like being horrible to us, you can tell by the look on his face whenever Mocha makes him do something. Julian has begged us more than once to just do as we're told so he doesn't have to be mean."

"Has he told you anything else? Like why he's in this line of business?"

"Nothing. As far as I can make out, they're both single because they never bring any women here, but then maybe they do in the middle of the night when we're asleep. As you know, the dorm's locked when the last one of those two goes to bed, so it's not like we can sneak out and listen at their doors, is it."

While there was the illusion the women could wander around the house whenever they wanted to, it had quickly vanished when the key had clicked in the lock that first night and she'd realised they'd effectively been caged. It worried her that without an escape route should a fire break out, they could all die in the dormitory if Julian or Mocha didn't rescue them in time.

"Have you ever thought about setting a fire?" she asked.

Fantasy raised her eyebrows. "What with?"

"Fair point." None of the kitchen appliances used gas for them to need a lighter or matches, but if they had, setting something alight meant they'd have to go outside—then they could run. A tea towel left on the electric hob would work.

But what if Mocha had a gun like that man at the ritual?

She imagined being gunned down and winced. "How come Candy seems so happy to stay here?"

"She's had a really, really shitty life. To her, this house and the rituals are heaven."

"She might not be saying that with the new crap we've got to do."

"Hmm."

"How do you feel about visiting the disciples at home?"

"If it gives us more of a chance to escape, then I'll do whatever it takes," Fantasy said. "It's true what I said, I do miss my Amazon deliveries, and going out for a coffee whenever I want, opening a window whenever I want. Here, we're just property, but we deserve to be paid for losing our liberty and working for the High Priest."

"I think it's remiss of them to talk about that in front of us—to talk about any of it. Tara told me everything about this place, as much as she could remember anyway, so you'd think they'd keep things a secret as much as possible in case one of us does the same thing as her and gets away."

"I bet they told us she'd died to make us think it was useless to try and escape."

"Probably, and who knows, they might have had to tell you that because that's a lie they also told the High Priest." Empress wouldn't let Fantasy know she'd had some information from Julian, but it didn't stop her from suggesting it as though she'd thought of it herself. "Just think, if they've been put in charge of looking after four women at a time and one of them got away, out of a moving car no less, and then they told their boss the woman was alive and could potentially have told the police all about them... I can't see them still being alive, can you?"

Fantasy shook her head. "No, HP would have them offed. So what's your plan? I can tell you've got one."

"I'm going to make Julian really trust me. I'll get him to help us escape."

"I can't see him doing that; he does whatever Mocha tells him to."

"I'll be persuasive."

Fantasy's eyes lit up. "That could work, but it's going to take time."

"Well, we have a lot of it, so we may as well put it to good use." Empress opened the bathroom door to check the other two weren't in the bedroom, then she closed it again. "By the way, I agree with you, I think Pearl's a snitch, and maybe Candy, too, because she's just a bit too okay with this situation for my liking. Either she's a plant to make us think that we ought to be submissive like her, or she genuinely does like it here. If she's not pretending, then I'm worried about her mental health."

"It's crossed my mind, too, that she could be a bit airy-fairy up top so she doesn't quite understand what's being asked of her. There's something not quite right in her acceptance—and it was pretty quick. Have you been able to contact your colleagues?"

"I sent a message to let my boss know I'm at this house and that I participated in a ritual. He apologised for losing the SUV on the housing estate, told me to say safe, that kind of thing."

"What about sending him a ping of your location?"

"It's not that kind of phone. It's a very basic burner, and think about it, they'd be able to get a location after I sent those texts, but he said there was no ping happening. I think they've got some kind of device here that stops the phone use being picked up."

"Then we need to persuade Julian to let us outside in the daytime so we can see if there are any visible landmarks that you can message your boss about, plus the device might work out there. We can't stay here forever."

"I doubt we would anyway. There'll come a time when we're too old for what they want us to do, and then they'll probably kill us."

Fantasy turned to the sink and ran the cold water, splashing it over her eyes and cheeks.

"Where were you three taken from?" Empress asked.

Fantasy faced her again. "I was taken from outside the Noodle; Candy was a road away from Kitchen Street; Pearl said she'd been round the corner from The Angel. She stood outside the graveyard gates."

"All from the Cardigan Estate," Empress mused. "Could that be significant? The industrial estate's also there, so it might be Mocha's stomping ground when he isn't here or it's somewhere he used to hang around as a kid—he prefers to work on familiar territory." She'd test whether Julian had lied to her about his reason for being here. "Are Julian and Mocha mates or something, or did the High Priest just make them work together?"

"I don't know, but if I had to guess, I'd say they were strangers before."

It was looking more and more likely that Julian had chosen Empress for someone to offload to. His job was a pretty shit one, ensuring women were incarcerated inside a building, and then when he had to ferry them to the ritual sites, and in the future the residential addresses, he'd have to make sure none of them ran away. The taxi had been mentioned as a means to get to the homes of the red disciples, but how could Julian keep track of four women without losing one, or more?

She'd ask him tomorrow if they had a quiet moment on their own.

"We'd better go to bed like we said." Fantasy dried her face and left the bathroom.

Empress followed, her mind going a mile a minute on how she'd get the women to freedom, and Julian, *once she'd had a measure of what the residential visits would be like. She dreaded to think what was in store for them, but if enduring this meant they could win their freedom, then she was all for it.*

She'd just have to lie back and think of England.

DS LITTLE: I HEARD A WOMAN CONTACTED THE POLICE WITH INFORMATION. SHE GAVE THE LAST RITUAL LOCATION, YES? CHECK GRASS IN THE CLEARING FOR DNA. PLEASE DON'T ASK ME TO SPELL OUT WHY.

DI TAYLOR: YOU'RE TEACHING ME TO SUCK EGGS. ALREADY DONE. WHAT'S THE SCORE NOW?

DS LITTLE: RITUALS ARE BEING STOPPED. WE'LL BE TAKEN TO MEN'S HOUSES FOR SEX INSTEAD.

DI TAYLOR: SHIT. THE LORRY USED, WHERE IS IT KEPT?

DS LITTLE: WE WERE BROUGHT BACK TO THE HOUSE IN IT, BUT NO IDEA IF IT'S KEPT HERE OR TAKEN AWAY.

DI TAYLOR: DO YOU KNOW ANYTHING MORE ABOUT THIS HIGH PRIEST CHARACTER OTHER THAN WHAT TARA TOLD US?

She went on to tell him about her discussion with Julian.

DI Taylor: Do you think that's a likely story or is he really in the same boat as you?

DS Little: I actually believe him.

DI Taylor: We'll look through the MisPer list, see if a Julian comes up.

DS Little: He's very worried about his wife and sons. If you find them, any chance you can secretly get them away to safety?

DI Taylor: It's certainly high on my priority list.

DS Little: Someone's moving about in the bedroom. Got to go.

DI Taylor: Stay safe.

Chapter Twenty

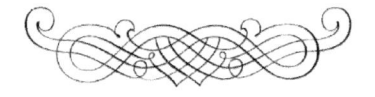

The house, painted light pink, was a fucking eyesore. George stared at it in disbelief as Greg parked outside. Prior to coming here, they'd gone home to put on beards and glasses. The black tracksuits had stayed, and they'd chosen shaggy shoulder-length wigs rather than long ones. George had opted for his usual ginger, Greg the blond. They'd used their little van.

"What sort of reception do you reckon we're going to get?" Greg asked.

"Going by the house, which stands out a mile compared to all the others in the street, she's perhaps a show-off or isn't afraid to display a gregarious side, which means we might be dealing with an overconfident person."

"Hmm. Feeny wasn't exactly giving us any pointers on her personality, was he."

"Maybe he barely knows her or not at all." George eyed the closed blinds on the windows. It was only the afternoon, so had she gone away? Gone to bed? Had Feeny had the last laugh and sent them somewhere the resident wasn't even home?

It dawned on George then. "I get what he's done."

"Who?"

"Feeny, who else? If you remember, Fantasy said Mocha went to his mum's house every Sunday for dinner. It's Sunday."

"But it's past lunchtime when you'd normally have a roast, so wouldn't he have fucked off by now?"

"Weren't you listening? She said most of the time he didn't get back until late. Maybe this was Feeny's way of dropping Mocha in the shit without him actually saying he'd be here, so therefore, technically, he hadn't grassed him up."

"Why would he care about grassing him up anyway? As the High Priest, he seemed to have them all over a barrel. They were dancing to his tune, not the other way around. The only thing that bothers me is whether Feeny wasn't really the High Priest, he just pretended to be for the real one. Which would make sense that a kid like him couldn't pull off a stunt like this."

"But he could. Look at the way all these influencers on social media are raking in the cash. Look how clever they are to come up with half the shit they do to get views. Feeny tapped into something, ran with it, and it just so happened to make him a fortune. Hang on a second while I send a message to the crew. We need his flat cleared out and someone to pick up his electronics. He could have a list of red disciples and watchers. I'd like to have a word with everyone involved."

"He might have been clever enough not to keep a list. He didn't even have a phone on him when he was picked up."

"Maybe he did and when he realised Moody had come to collect him, he dropped it in the bin in the gents. I'll send a message for someone to go and have a look."

While George did that, Greg got out of the car and paced beside it. George sent another message for Mason to look into Mocha's mother, see if she was anyone they needed to revisit later down the line. She could be in on this shit. He checked all the other incoming messages and found one that was proper interesting.

COLIN: MORE FROM DETECTIVE RUNNING THE CASE. UNDERCOVER COPPER HAS MADE CONTACT, SAYING JULIAN'S BEEN FORCED TO WORK FOR THE HP. HE WAS ABDUCTED FROM HIS FLAT AND TAKEN TO THE HOUSE. THREATS HAVE BEEN MADE. IF HE DOESN'T COMPLY, HIS FAMILY WILL BE KILLED. HE HAS NO CLUE THEY'RE SAFE, POOR BASTARD. ALSO, THERE ARE VIDEOS HE WOULDN'T WANT THEM TO SEE, SO HE'S AGREED TO DO WHATEVER HE'S TOLD. FROM WHAT I CAN GATHER, THE HIGH PRIEST HAS INFORMATION ON EVERY DISCIPLE AND WATCHER.

GG: DOESN'T SURPRISE ME. CHEERS FOR THE INFO.

George joined Greg and whispered what he'd found out.

"Quite the clever little bastard, Feeny," Greg said.

"I bet all those videos and whatever will be on any electronics the crew find."

George led the way up the garden path. He rang the bell first then tapped on the door, telling himself to be calm and collected to begin with to see how things were. He'd soon change his tune if she gave them any gyp.

The door opened, and a woman in her mid-forties, blonde hair in a ponytail, her clothing indicating she'd perhaps been doing some aerobics, stood there frowning at them. She gave them an up-and-down appraisal, then made eye contact with George. "Did my son send you here? I knew something was wrong when he told me he wasn't coming round for dinner today. He's always here for dinner on a Sunday, it's our *day*, and unless he's ill, then something's up."

"What's your name, love?" George asked.

"What do you want to know for?"

"So I know I've got the right person."

She frowned harder. "Oh God, are you coppers who dress like criminals so you can entrap people? I've seen it on the telly. Has my son done something wrong and you've come round to give me the bad news?" She laid a hand on her chest above the low scooped neckline of her vest top.

"Why would you think your son had done something wrong?"

"Well, you police like to pin things on innocent people."

"I'd say it's more likely that you're aware your son might be the type to commit a crime which is why your mind went straight to that."

"Look, what do you want?"

"Your name."

"Show me a warrant card first."

"We don't have one because we're not police officers."

"So who the fuck are you? Thugs? Does he owe you money, is that it?"

"He owes us an explanation as to what he's been up to lately, so if you wouldn't mind telling us where he is, then we'll leave you be."

"Who are you first?"

George leaned forward to whisper in her ear, "The Brothers. I'm George, and you're sorely testing my patience." He pulled back just in time to see her expression, eyes wide, mouth an 'O'.

"Jesus fucking wept... You'd better come in. I don't want any trouble from you two, thank you very much. I'll stick the kettle on and you can tell me all about it." She turned and walked down the hallway.

George glanced at Greg, smiled, and went inside.

"I had a feeling he was up to something," she said as soon as they stepped foot in the kitchen.

George gave the room a quick scan. No table and chairs for them to sit, all the mod cons, and she was the kind who favoured putting everything in transparent containers and labelling them with swirly font. The shelves above her toaster contained porridge, granola, split peas and the like, and on the worktop above the washing machine, those bead things that make your clothes smell nice, liquid pods, and a glass bottle of what he assumed was blue fabric softener—there wasn't a label on that one.

"And I told him I didn't want him bringing trouble to my door—he's got one of those faces people don't forget. I remember when he was little and he nicked some chocolate down the corner shop and said he hadn't done it, but when I marched him down there to give it back to the shopkeeper, as soon as he saw us—the shopkeeper, I mean—he launched into a fucking tirade about him robbing a Mars. The kettle's not long boiled. Do you want tea or coffee?"

George spotted a coffee machine and pointed to that. "Um, what's your son's name?"

She paused putting a pod in the machine and stared at him. "Are you taking the piss? First you don't know my name, now you don't know my son's. Are you even in the right place? Are you even the twins?"

Greg took his beard and wig off and popped the glasses in his pocket. He returned the wig and beard to their former places, smirking at her gawping at him. "Now we've got one question answered, I'll respond to the others. We don't know your name because we weren't told it, only your address, and the person who's looking into who you are hasn't got back to us yet. Please don't test me. We're tired, we're hungry, and George will soon get fucking grumpy. As for not knowing your son's name, we have a nickname, but I doubt very much that's what you had put on his birth certificate."

"Mocha," she said, putting a cup under the spout and setting the machine off.

"Why's he called that?"

"No other reason than he likes the drink." She handed George what appeared to be an espresso; there was fuck all in the cup. Maybe she didn't want them to hang around for long. "Bloody Nora, I've used the wrong pod. Give it back here." She put the cup under the spout and loaded a cappuccino pod. "This will be double the strength now, but you did say you were tired... Anyway, I'm Laura Stokes, and my son's Peter Beard—I didn't marry his father, who's fuck knows where before you ask. What's my boy done?"

George told her while she sorted all their drinks and acted as though he hadn't just told her that Peter was involved in an illegal sex racket. Maybe it was her way of coping with what she was hearing—keeping her face blank, her emotions in check, not even uttering any sounds of disgust, although it was obvious she hadn't known about any of this bollocks until now. At one point she leaned her lower back on the worktop and tucked her hands under her armpits, either self-soothing or needing to hide the trembling of her fingers.

"I'll say that I thought my kid would do a fair few things to make money, but not that. Those poor women... I've seen them on the news, they've been the main stories for months, the three who're missing. We even talked about it over dinner last weekend, for fuck's sake."

"What was his reaction?"

"He said he felt sorry for them and reckoned they'd be long gone, like, they're dead. He said something about them being too hot to handle, and I just took it that he was imagining the amount of press their disappearances had got and how the kidnapper or whatever you want to call them had probably got rid of them rather than risk holding on to them. I honest to God didn't think any more of it. Now you're telling me *he* was involved, *he* was the one to abduct them. Who the hell are the High Priest and this Julian character?"

"The High Priest is a kid called Feeny. It's hard to believe, and going by the amount of time this has been in operation, he's got to have been a teenager when he started it."

Laura shook her head. "The kids these days… They're scary, the amount they can do compared to us lot when we were younger, aren't they."

"Hmm." The phone went off. George read the message.

MASON: SHE'S CLEAN.

That was a relief. "Do you know where the boarded-up house is?"

She laughed. "He said he rented a house with a few other people, they split the rent, and that's why I could never go over there to visit because the others didn't want parents snooping round. He wasn't lying, I suppose, he *did* live with other people, just that they all seem to be there under duress. He did mention a Julian, said he had to bully him to get him to do what he wanted. I took it that he meant his share of the housework and stuff like that, but obviously he's been forcing the poor bloke to look after the women." She sighed. "I'm struggling to get my head around it. It's one thing to think your kid could nick a few things, but this…" She jolted as if a thought had given her a shock. "What if *he's* being forced as well?"

"That's something we'll be asking him. So, do you know the address?"

"I don't know the exact one, but I know it's along the Caridean Road, you know, the one by Daffodil Woods. I was with Peter once when we drove past it—we we're going to Essex to do a bit of shopping, and he pointed out that's where he lived. I remember saying it was a good job there were a few of them living there, otherwise it'd be too expensive for him on his own. It's a very big house. There were shutters on the windows, and it had a black front door. There's a long driveway."

"Did you ever see him flush with cash?"

"No."

"So he was either hiding how much he earned from you or it fits with your idea that he might have been forced into working for the High Priest. Mocha and Julian might be just like the women and only get the house to live in and food to eat as their payment."

She appeared to latch on to that, grasping on to the hope that her son wasn't that much of a deviant that he could do what he'd done to those women of his own free will. "He'd never kill anyone unless he had no choice. I can't see him doing any of it, to be honest, or maybe I just don't want to. Maybe he really *is* a bastard but doesn't show me that side of himself."

"Can you do me a favour and try ringing him to see where he is? I don't have to tell you to keep your mouth shut about us two being here, do I?"

"No. He might be my son, but if he's done something wrong then he needs to be held accountable for it. I don't want him killed. I've heard you make people disappear, so couldn't you just banish him instead? Make him leave London? If he was forced to do what he's done, surely you could give him some leeway."

"It'll depend on his attitude when we speak to him. If it's obvious he's been coerced into this, then we can be lenient."

She reached for her phone on the side and prodded the speaker button. Her call rang out. "Oh God, what if that priest person's got hold of him?"

"He's dead."

"Shit... You two?"

George nodded.

Laura took a deep breath. "Go and do what you've got to do. I love my son, but if he's willingly done this stuff..." She scrubbed at her face to rub away tears. "If he's got to go the same way as the priest, just promise me you'll make it quick."

They finished drinking their coffees, Laura perhaps contemplating her son's fate, George doing the same. Fantasy had mentioned Julian as the only man who didn't belong in that house, nor did he seem suited to the kind of work he was expected to do. Mocha, on the other hand, had been portrayed as a bully, but George wasn't about to tell Laura that.

"If we have to make him disappear," he said, "then you must understand you have to keep it to yourself, the reason why he hasn't come to see you again."

She nodded, her lips wobbling. "Do you think I want people knowing what my boy's been up to? And do you think I want you two coming back to finish me off because I blabbed? What's going on is awful, really bloody awful, but excuse me for being selfish and worrying about myself and how I'll have to carry on knowing all this, possibly without my son coming for a visit ever again. I feel bad for those women, I really do, but if you don't mind, I'm going to wallow in self-pity until I know the outcome. You will tell me, won't you, that he's not coming home?"

"Isn't it best that you're oblivious, that you think he's been banished and we've told him not to contact you again? Fooling yourself like that is better than facing the truth, isn't it?"

"Oh, just go."

"If you change your mind and decide to warn him, it'll make no difference in the end. We'll find him wherever he goes, and he'll face a grilling from us and the consequences of what he's been up to, regardless. All you'd be doing is delaying the inevitable. If he can convince us he's been forced, then there's no problem. He'll turn up here, asking you for a plate of food, and Bob's your uncle, everything's sorted."

"But it might not go that way."

"No, it might not, but that's the chance you'll have to take."

Chapter Twenty-One

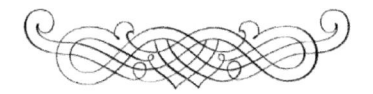

The first night where they'd be going to the house of a red disciple had arrived. No one could relax all day. Even Julian had a case of the wobbles, although he did well not to let the others see it. He'd whispered to Empress that he had to pull this off without a hitch or he'd be in trouble.

Now, standing in the hallway of the big house, Empress managed to squeeze his arm as a gesture of reassurance, and he nodded his thanks to her. She sensed something wasn't right. Maybe he had info that he hadn't passed on to them yet, or maybe she was picking up his unease at doing something different to the rituals. Whatever it was, it transferred into her as a ball of anxiety in her stomach. But how could she expect him to fully open up to her when they hadn't known each other that long? It was ridiculous of her to think they'd become thick as thieves.

Each woman held their blindfold. It gave Empress the creeps how they appeared to accept this was how it was going to be—and something still didn't sit right with that *either. There was only Julian, Mocha was fuck knows where, so how was he going to control them all?*

With his back to the front door, Julian took a deep breath. "As always, there will be men out there in the dark, waiting with their guns should you decide to run."

Empress lowered her eyebrows at Fantasy—why hadn't any of them passed that snippet on to her? "Men? Guns? I wasn't aware of that. Isn't that a bit much?"

Julian sighed and glanced at each one of them in turn until his attention finally rested on Empress. "I'm sorry that your housemates didn't give you all of the information—like they were told to." He shook his head at the other three. *"I won't tell Mocha you failed to follow his instructions, but what were you thinking? Empress could have made a run for it and then got shot. You know it's my job to keep you safe, yet you were willing to lose another one, like we lost Tara?"*

Mumbled apologies followed along with dipped heads.

"Just so we're all clear, here are the rules again. We leave the house and get straight into the SUV. You put on your blindfolds. You do not take them off until you're told to. We've already been through the new rules regarding visiting the disciples' homes—but what you haven't been informed about yet is that when we arrive, men will be in the vicinity with weapons, so if you think of running at that point, then you'd better think again."

"Bloody hell," Candy said, "I've told you I never want to run."

"But there are three others besides you who might," Julian said, "who probably want to get home to their old lives. Basically, whenever you try to run, you'll get

shot. Even if it looks like we're in a situation where there are no gunmen around, don't be fooled."

Empress twigged that this was all a load of bollocks; this was his way of controlling them. There were no gunmen. The existence of snipers was nothing but a threat, something to make them behave themselves. Doubt had been planted in their heads—could they risk running when someone could shoot them?

"Not if we try to get out of the car on the way like Tara did," Fantasy said. "Unless we're being followed by gunmen, who's going to shoot us then?"

"There's no way you'll be able to get out of the car, Mocha's made sure of that, he's learned by his mistakes." Julian stared at her. "And use your loaf. I'll shoot you, just like Mocha shot Tara."

Empress prayed Fantasy wouldn't give the game away by blurting that Tara was alive. It was a pressure-cooker environment in this tense moment, the pair of them having a battle of wills, glaring, seeing who'd be the first to break.

Empress wondered about four women sitting in the back of the large vehicle, having the chance to overpower Julian who'd be driving. It'd be easy to cover his eyes so he couldn't see and ended up crashing, then they could jump out and run across the fields to find help.

She said as much now in front of everyone.

"I mean, last time I went out we were put in the back of a lorry, so the car scenario is new to me, which means I'm unaware of the protocols there. I suppose you're going to say there are measures in place for if any of us decide to do you some damage."

Pearl smoothed over one of her fingernails. "Mocha told me there's now a partition between the front and back seats."

He really had thought of everything.

"Any more questions?" Julian asked.

With no answer, he pulled a couple of chains out of his pocket with handcuffs on each end. He handed one to Pearl and one to Fantasy. Pearl clipped the handcuff to her wrist, and Candy did the same to hers, joining them together. Fantasy cuffed herself and Empress.

Julian took a gun out of his back pocket. "I don't want to have to use this, okay? Pearl and Candy first, please."

With the gun trained on them, he opened the front door and chivvied them outside, closing it behind him and leaving Empress and Fantasy indoors.

"They really are worried we're going to try to escape like Tara," Fantasy whispered. "We've never been chained together like this. You saw me sitting in the back of the SUV when we picked you up. I didn't have handcuffs on or anything, I just knew it was pointless trying to get away because Mocha had made a big point of locking us inside."

"Are there really men out there with guns? Have you ever seen them? It's not like we're ever going to know, is it, because it's so dark."

"I don't know, but I've never had the bottle to see if it's true."

The sound of a key sliding in the lock churned Empress' stomach. The door opened, and Julian poked his head around it.

"Come on," he said.

He stepped back to allow them out. The SUV had been parked so close to the front door that if they chose now to escape, by the time they scooted around it to run, he'd have gone round the other side and caught up with them.

The back door was open, and they got inside.

"Seat belts on, please."

Julian slammed the door and walked towards the driver's side.

"Well, this is new," Pearl said from the middle seats. "Being chained. I suppose we could look on the bright side and say that they really don't want to lose us because we're good at our jobs."

The joke fell flat.

"That might change tonight, though," Fantasy said. "If we've actually got to have sex with a disciple... Mocha could be waiting there to rate our performances. The High Priest might be there. Other disciples. Watchers."

Empress shuddered. "Do you think we'll have to service the client one after the other?"

"I expect we'll be in the same room all at the same time," Fantasy said. "But if no one else is there then it'd only be a disciple and Julian. There's four of us and two of them, so if we're all together then they can keep an eye on us better. It wouldn't surprise me if they have men with guns standing at the exits, though. I don't think any of us are going to get the chance to run away so we may as well not bother. I might just do what Candy's done and accept my lot." She sighed.

The engine started.

"Shit, blindfolds on," Candy said.

Empress glanced over to the door of the house to see what Julian had been hiding when she'd first arrived here. It was a plaque of some kind, but she couldn't make out what was on it because it was too dark. She covered her eyes, pissed off to find the blindfolds were different to when she'd worn one in the lorry. It moulded around her eyes so she wouldn't be able to peep. They'd probably changed them as an assurance to the red disciples that their home address wouldn't be compromised by spying women. Considering one of their number had confessed all to his wife, the others might well be jittery, although they couldn't be feeling too worried because they'd agreed to this new way of doing things. They must be desperate to get their jollies if they were willing to risk Julian, Mocha, and the High Priest knowing where they lived. Then again, they probably already did. This wasn't the kind of outfit where people walked in off the street, no questions asked. The men would have been vetted, their pasts poked into.

Earlier, Julian had told her why he'd been threatened and forced to work for them. He was a former red disciple, and there was evidence he'd participated in a ritual. Photographs of him without his mask on. Photos of him inside the stone circle with a woman. A short video. He'd got a dose of the guilts and backed out after only one ritual, saying the remorse was too much and he should never have cheated on his wife. When disciples signed up to play the game, they agreed on five rituals. The High Priest had let Julian walk away after only one, but with the threat that he owed the High Priest who'd come calling for payment at a later date. But instead of asking for *the four thousand pounds, he'd chosen him as the women's jailer.*

Was him participating in a ritual enough to keep Julian's mouth shut, though, and to ensure his compliance? It didn't seem enough of a threat. If Empress broke it down to the basics, it was just an elaborate hookup with other women, a man cheating on his wife; it didn't mean the end of the world. But what if he still loved his wife? He may not want her to know just how much of a naughty boy he'd been. She could be one of those who wasn't into kink, so a ritual would sound alien and perhaps dirty to her, in turn making **him** *dirty.*

So he'd opted to do this job rather than her find out?

He'd let her and their sons go through the pain of his disappearance rather than say he'd played with his dick by some stones?

Really?

No, there had to be more to this. When Empress was with him and she could see his face, she believed every word he said, but when she was away from him and had time to reflect, she became unsure, questioning everything he'd told her, asking herself if this was just some stupid little story he'd made up to lure her in for whatever reason.

She dared to raise her blindfold. Through the partition glass, she caught his eye in the rearview mirror. He shook his head to tell her to put it back on.

As she lowered the blindfold, she caught sight of a service station.

Something to tell the boss later.

The taxi idea had been abandoned, the SUV used for the whole of the journey. Maybe Empress' observation that blindfolds would stand out to a cab driver had been heeded—reluctantly, or had Mocha thought she had a good head on her shoulders with her input? She had yet to get to know him, he didn't mix with them much at the house, preferring to read in the library or lock himself away in the office. She doubted she'd be able to get him talking like Julian, so maybe she shouldn't bother even trying.

They were allowed to take their blindfolds off before they got out of the car, and Empress could see why. There was nothing out there but a high brick wall with a dark-blue wooden gate in the middle. Light from behind the wall lit up a huge tree. The SUV was parked in a secluded tarmac area, like a place for staff to put their cars. Was this disciple rich? Did he live in a big house behind the wall?

Julian reached in to unlock the cuffs. Several instances presented themselves where one of them could get out and run, but with the darkness so black beyond the light, there was no telling where they'd be heading and who could be lurking with a gun.

Everyone had chosen to behave and get out when told. The gate opened, and three men came over, all of them holding guns. They each gripped the arm of a woman, Julian taking hold of Empress', and marched them through into a small garden tucked away down the side of a building. Led across the grass, Empress took in all the sights: the men with guns had those creepy white masks on. To the right, a summerhouse, a little pond, a wooden bench, potted plants. It was as if this space had been designed for someone to enjoy alone, a secret haven.

A right turn brought them out to the front of what could only be described as a manor set in its own grounds and well away from any lights in the distance. A sweeping circular driveway. Empress clocked a stone in the lintel above the front door: BUILT *1865. She memorised it to send to Taylor later. She hadn't brought her phone with her, not when she didn't know what was expected of her, not really. She might not be able to get the mobile out of her knickers in time before someone spotted it, but now she'd thought about it, she should have risked it. She could have sent a message, and it would have pinged a mast.*

The men with guns stepped back, standing in a semi-circle so if anyone ran, they'd be caught. Julian let Empress go and moved to the front door, knocking. It opened, but no one stood there. Maybe the disciple had been told to stand behind it. Everyone filed inside, Julian at the rear, and Empress caught sight of something red. She turned fully to look at the door, and a red disciple, masked, came out from behind it. He or she let the gunmen in, locked the door, then walked up the stairs. Julian gestured for Pearl, Candy, Fantasy, and Empress to follow, then he tailed them at the back.

What followed was a ritual performed in a bedroom but with no High Priest, no other disciples, and no watchers. But the music made an appearance. They lay in a line on a super-king bed, Julian standing with his back against the door, eyes closed while the disciple pranced around in their cloak.

Empress shut her mind off after that.

DS LITTLE: TAKEN TO LARGE MANOR HOUSE IN BLACK SUV. SECLUDED. COUNTRYSIDE. BUILT IN 1865. CAUGHT SIGHT OF SERVICE STATION ON THE WAY. THINK IT MIGHT BE BRANDWOOD? I'M BACK AT USUAL HOUSE FOR NIGHT NOW.

DI TAYLOR: GOOD INTEL, THANKS. ARE YOU HOLDING UP OKAY?

DS LITTLE: YES, I HAVE AN ALLY. WOMAN CALLING HERSELF FANTASY. STREET NAME ON THE OUTSIDE IS BLUEBELL—WILL PUMP FOR MORE INFO ON REAL NAME. SHE WAS TAKEN FROM OUTSIDE THE NOODLE PUB. WHAT ABOUT YOU, GOT ANYTHING FOR ME?

DI TAYLOR: HITS ON DNA LEFT AT LAST RITUAL SCENE—TWO OF THE THREE MEN WERE IN POLICE DATABASE AND HAVE BEEN QUESTIONED, BUT NEITHER ARE TALKING ABOUT THE RITUALS. HAVE FOUND JULIAN'S WIFE. ACCORDING TO HER, HE DISAPPEARED ONE DAY, THEN NO WORD. HAVE EXPLAINED HIS CIRCUMSTANCES. SHE'S GONE INTO HIDING WITH HER BOYS.

DS LITTLE: RIGHT. GOT TO SWITCH PHONE OFF TO PRESERVE BATTERY. CAN'T RISK CHARGING IT YET. I'M STILL TOO NEW HERE TO TAKE ANY CHANCES.

DI Taylor: Thanks for the update. Will try to find manor based on possible Brandwood sighting. Keep safe.

Chapter Twenty-Two

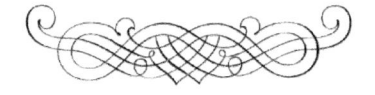

Pearl sat in the kitchen with the others and eyed Empress. There was something off about her. *Or maybe I'm just jealous.* In order to accept her role here, Pearl had tried to make herself queen of the girls, the one Mocha would notice and take to his bed, so eventually, he'd trust her so much he'd slip up and put his keys down where she could steal them. She pretended to like it here, pretended a lot of things, but in reality, her only goal was escaping.

Empress had made dinner—spaghetti bolognese rather than a roast. Everyone had agreed they weren't feeling chicken, potatoes, and vegetables with gravy today. They were all too tired to muck about for hours in the kitchen after last night—Mocha had said they could abandon the Sunday cleaning rota just this once. They'd almost finished their meals, everyone eating without speaking. It was eerie, like there had been a death or something.

That shitshow at Jerry's... Fucking hell. God, that had been her chance to get away right there, but she'd stupidly grabbed Candy and gone out the back with Julian and Empress. She'd seen Fantasy going out the front and wished she could have gone with her, but she'd convinced herself it was a trick, that Mocha had told Empress to pretend there were blue lights outside so he could see who was loyal or not. Pearl had visions of him waiting out the front and catching Fantasy, taking her back to the house then killing her in front of everyone to remind them all that his threats weren't empty. The fear of that had overridden

Pearl's desire to run away. She'd only do it when she could see exactly where she was going and no surprises could jump out at her.

Mocha had checked the news, and it had been an eye-opener. It was out there that other women had been abducted—more than just the three dead ones behind the barn. Pearl's real name had been featured, but she'd kept her mouth shut that it was her. Her neighbour, Bunty, had reported her as missing. Mocha hadn't batted an eyelid, he hadn't asked any of them who Miranda Stevens was, which had clued Pearl in that he *didn't* know her true identity or where she lived—he'd just made out he did so she behaved herself here.

The police had known an awful lot about what went on in this house, so Fantasy must have blabbed. Pearl had to disguise her disappointment earlier when they'd all sat discussing it. She could be free right now, put into witness protection or something, or at least hidden away in a safe house until the High Priest had been caught—because let's face it, he was the only real threat. She could wrap Mocha around her little finger even more if she had to, and as for Julian, he sometimes pretended to be gruff, but he was soft as shit underneath.

Despite everything that had happened, they were a family. A dysfunctional one, but a family all the same, and wasn't that weird for her to know she was going to miss all this when everyone went their separate ways? *If* they did. Would she hang around with Mocha if they were all free? Knowing her, she probably would — she'd always been desperate to be loved — but she reckoned he was only using her for the time being; she was there and convenient, the prettiest out of them all, even if she did say so herself.

She thought about her life before she'd been abducted. She'd only been working on the Cardigan Estate for a week, having been told she couldn't work on Proust without permission. *That* Estate where she lived was a weird one, where the leader expected you to apply for a permit if you wanted to do a job that wasn't exactly the norm. You were given a lanyard to wear that you showed to whoever asked to see it. Fuck that. Yes, she was supposed to have approached the twins and discussed protection money or to be placed on a proper patch, but she hadn't got around to it.

If she ever got out of here, she hoped she'd still have her house to go back to.

She tuned in to the conversation going on around her. Mocha got up and paced. He'd been agitated ever since news of the police at Jerry's house had come up on social media.

"What's the matter?" she asked him.

"I know we've already talked about it earlier, but it's *really* bugging me: who phoned the police last night?"

Pearl took a deep breath. "Other than Julian, who didn't have his phone out because I'd have seen it and I'd have heard him talking, no one else could have got in contact with the police and told them where we were. Jerry was too occupied, if you catch my drift. It can't have been one of us girls, because how could we even know where we were to pass that information on? We'd been blindfolded on the journey, like usual, and we don't have mobiles. So who's left?"

Julian looked at Empress.

Oh yeah, she went to the toilet...

"Does Jerry have a house phone?" Pearl asked.

"Not that I saw," Julian said.

"Why?" Mocha frowned.

"Because Empress went to the loo. She could have used it..."

"But even if I did, I didn't know the address," Empress said. "Like you've already pointed out, we had blindfolds on, so how could I have told the police where to go?"

Candy put her fork down. "They could trace the call. Check the number against who pays the bill."

"But it wasn't me," Empress said, "so it's a moot point. I went for a wee, end of."

Pearl scoffed. "Who else is there? Can you see the High Priest shitting all over his own business?" She stared at Mocha.

"You cheeky cow," he said. "You reckon it was *me*? I get how it *looks* like it's me, but I'm telling you, it sodding well isn't. I've even wondered whether it was the High Priest myself, but that would be stupid. Or it *could* be Jerry—he's been threatened like all the other disciples and watchers. Maybe he got sick of worrying whether he'd get another visit to remind him of the rules and what's at stake."

Candy shook her head. "Jerry was well naffed off that we were leaving him because he said he'd paid for an hour."

"That could have just been him playing a part," Julian said. "Making out he was arsey when it was him who'd phoned the police before we'd even arrived. For all we know he could have wanted to back out of the disciple deal and the only way he could do it was by getting the coppers to come round."

Mocha flopped onto one of the chairs and scrubbed a hand over his face. He told Pearl things whenever they were in bed — whether they were the truth or not she didn't know — and according to him, he had no choice, he *had* to do this job and live in this house. He hadn't gone into detail about why, just muttered about them all being in the same boat, kind of, and the puppet master High Priest pulled all their strings. She hadn't pressed it at the time, just stroked his belly while he'd talked to make him think she was a decent listener and someone worth keeping around. But now she wished she'd asked questions. Maybe he would have answered them, maybe he wouldn't, but at least she'd have given it a good try.

"All I know is that it wasn't me and I've got a clear conscience," she said.

Julian shifted the conversation to childhoods and how theirs had been. When it came to her turn, Pearl didn't reveal anything, but Empress said:

"My parents preferred the drink and their friends over their child, so I spent a lot of time next door with a single woman who had eight kids. It was bloody chaotic there, but at least I felt safe and cared for."

"That's bloody sad," Mocha said.

"No sadder than you allowing us to be held here. Like my parents, you made a decision, regardless of who gets hurt in the process." Empress shrugged. "We all do shit that affects others, so I'm not picking fault, just saying."

Mocha levelled a stare at her. "Some of us don't have the luxury of making a decision, it's made for us."

Here was Pearl's chance to find stuff out, stuff she'd regretted not probing for previously. "Do you want to talk about that? Because to me, it sounds like you don't want to keep us locked up, but you have to."

Mocha glanced at Julian, then back to Pearl. "The High Priest calls the shots. We just make sure things go the way he wants."

Pearl wasn't about to reveal to the others that he'd kind of said as much to her before. She glanced around. Julian's eyebrows lowered. Was this the first time he was hearing this? Why was Mocha confessing now when he'd been so closed off to the group in the past? Was it because the police were involved and he needed to curry favour? He'd been horrible to them all, so was he panicking that if there was a raid here, he'd go down for a longer stretch because everyone would give statements saying he was a bastard?

"So you couldn't say no?" Candy asked him. "Like, he told you to keep us here and you had no choice?"

Mocha inhaled, his nostrils flaring. "Let's just say I have to live here and deal with everything, otherwise my mum gets hurt."

Pearl gasped—she hadn't been expecting that answer. "Christ, I'm sorry."

"It's the same for me, except my wife and kids will get hurt." Julian looked at Mocha—was that a dare in his eyes? A 'Don't you even try to stop me from telling my side of things, too'? "I wouldn't be here if it wasn't for my choices—ones used against me now. I'm being blackmailed. There are photos, a video…"

"So *that's* why you've always been nice to us," Pearl said. "Because it's not in your nature to be nasty." She stared at Mocha. "So how come *you've* been a wanker sometimes?"

"I was told to play the bad guy." Mocha stood, pacing again. "I don't want my mother to die, so here I am."

"Take charge. Get your mother safe," Empress said, "then we'll go to the police."

Pearl barked out a laugh. "Ha! I bet you *are* the police. You act well dodgy."

Empress frowned at her. "Eh?"

Mocha stopped and faced the table. "You what?"

"She's lying," Empress said on a sigh. "It could look like I'm a copper because of the amount of questions I was asking, but fucking hell, who *wouldn't* ask questions if they'd been brought here and told all this shit? It wouldn't be normal if I didn't."

Mocha nodded. "Hmm, I'll give you that."

Empress shrugged. "Do what you like. I've got nothing to hide."

Pearl sniffed. *I think you do…*

Chapter Twenty-Three

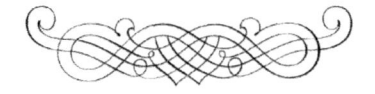

The following visits to disciple houses were different from the first. Many lived in smaller homes, though they were no less posh. One or two were what Empress considered 'normal', your average place with average things inside—it just showed you didn't have to be seen *as rich to be able to afford five stints at*

being a disciple. And it wasn't just Saturday nights anymore but every night, and several clients.

Weeks had passed—Empress had been able to charge her phone without detection. Taylor was still no further forward in discovering where the house was, or the manor they'd visited. She was stuck, unable to do anything but get closer to Julian and assure Fantasy that police operations sometimes took months, so to sit tight.

Empress had made the right move in continuing to talk to Julian because he made sure she didn't get violated at any of the disciples' houses. She thanked her lucky stars, because previous to that, she'd had to go along with whatever she was told. Now she was only used for titillation; she had to float about in flowing nightdresses and dance around to that creepy music, waving her arms, going close to the customer then darting back quickly so they couldn't touch her. Julian had said, when the others complained that Empress had an easy deal, that it was a working strategy, one approved of by Mocha, so they'd stick to it. Empress played the part of the High Priestess, an unobtainable fantasy.

Tonight they were on their way to Jerry's house, and for once she'd taken the phone. Empress only knew his name because she'd eavesdropped on Julian's *conversation with Mocha this morning. Mocha had warned him the house was in a residential street in a rough part of the Cardigan Estate, so Julian would need to be more careful—people there were apparently nosy. Julian had asked why they were taking the risk, then. Mocha had said the High Priest wanted the session to go ahead.*

He wanted the money more like.

The journey proceeded as usual, the women chained together. When they arrived, the handcuffs were released. Empress quickly lifted her blindfold. Julian had parked right by the bloody road sign declaring which street they were in. He caught her staring but didn't tell her to cover her eyes again. Did he trust her so much now that he'd let such a big thing go? She supposed, because she had no access to a phone (or so he thought), and she was scared of putting a foot wrong (again, so he thought), that she wouldn't be able to tell anyone where they were anyway. Jerry likely had a phone—didn't everyone?—but Julian always kept watch, so none of them would be able to use it secretly anyway.

Would there be men with guns here tonight, keeping guard? For the past few nights it had just been Julian, so he must think he had everything under control now. Or was he secretly getting it so eventually, they could all escape at the same time with minimal witnesses?

The number on the front door stood out as they approached it. She glanced at Fantasy who'd taken her blindfold off and also seemed to have clocked it. Pearl and Candy behaved like airheads, oblivious with their eyes covered—or was that an act? After all this time living with them, Empress still couldn't work that out. If they also had plans to escape, they were doing a good job of hiding it.

An older man opened the door—dishevelled-looking, as if he hadn't even bothered to shower. Greasy ginger hair. Empress' stomach churned. There should be rules about that. Disciples ought to at least be clean. Thank fuck she didn't have to touch him.

He led the way into an unkempt living room. Candy and Pearl took off their blindfolds. Jerry took a red cloak from the back of an armchair and put it on, undressing beneath it, eyeing Candy up and down, smiling—or was that leering?

Empress leaned towards Julian and whispered, "I need the loo."

He nodded.

She went upstairs and locked herself in the bathroom, taking the phone out. She sat on the toilet.

DS LITTLE: I'M AT A HOUSE. FOUR ALDING CLOSE. WHAT DO YOU WANT ME TO DO?

DI TAYLOR: STAY PUT. WE'LL BE WITH YOU SHORTLY. WHO'S THERE?

DS LITTLE: RESIDENT — A MALE CALLED JERRY. ME, THE THREE OTHER WOMEN, AND JULIAN.

DI TAYLOR: SEE YOU SOON.

Phone off, she put it back in her knickers, annoyed that the floaty nightie had too much material so she had to fight with it. She marvelled at how she'd dived into this role and stayed there for God knew how long, and for some reason she got a lump in her throat at the thought of it ending. She'd enjoyed living with other people. She laughed quietly. In the end, she'd done what she'd been advised and surrounded herself with others, and the therapist had been right — she did *feel less depressed.*

But it had *to end. She wanted to find and arrest the High Priest, but with Taylor on the way with other officers, it seemed he wasn't going to allow her to continue her undercover job any longer in order for her to do that. Did he think Julian would confess the things he knew about Mocha once he knew his family was safe? Like another address and his real name? Or would he keep quiet because he knew he might end up in prison?*

Fuck it. Should she blow this whole thing? It meant Julian would trust her even more if she did—she could tell him who she really was and that his wife and sons were in hiding. Maybe then he'd give her the info she needed about the High Priest so she could pass it on to Taylor. Julian could let them out of the house then escape himself.

Was she prepared to let him go, knowing what he'd done?

Taylor would bollock her if he knew what she had in mind, but she was going to make Julian's escape look genuine, that in a kerfuffle, he'd got away without her seeing him. Or they'd woken one morning with the dormitory door unlocked as well as the front door, no Julian in sight.

She'd work that out later. For now, she left the bathroom and, in the hallway downstairs, glanced into the living room. Julian looked her way, saw her expression of panic, and joined her.

"What's the matter?" he asked.

"Blue lights through the bathroom window." *She must be mad to want to do things her way and not Taylor's.*

Julian's eyes widened. "Fuck. They might not be coming here, though."

She tutted. "Do you want to stick around and find out?"

He peered into the living room. The women were on their knees around Jerry who sat in the armchair. "Jesus wept. Girls, we need to get a shift on."

Jerry's forehead creased. "Hang on a bloody minute, I've paid for an hour!"

"Coppers are on the way," Julian said. "We'll leave out the back."

He gestured for the women to follow him. Fantasy ran towards the front door, wrenching it open. Julian paused. Was he working out whether he could afford to let her go? Fantasy had always said she'd take the first chance she could get, and who'd blame her?

Julian shrugged. He gripped Pearl's and Candy's wrists. Empress followed them out through a side door in the kitchen. They hurried down a path to a gate at the bottom of the garden.

They jogged down a dark alley at the rear of the houses. Blue lights flashed between the homes in Alding Close. Fucking hell, it was go big or go home.

"Run!" Empress whisper-shouted. "Fucking run!"

They'd walked for ages and now stood in a lay-by behind thick pine trees, having made their way out of the housing estate, heads down, trudging along a field on the other side of a hedge so they were shielded from any cars on what amounted to a country road—probably the one that led to the boarded-up house.

"What are we doing here?" Candy asked.

"Waiting for Mocha to pick us up," Julian said. "I sent him a message."

"It had better be soon, because I'm freezing." Pearl rubbed her bare arms.

None of them, apart from Julian, were appropriately dressed. The chilly breeze kept billowing out Empress' nightie, pissing her off, her hands and feet numb. She was amazed Pearl hadn't made a run for it—so was she fixated on Mocha and had plans to be his permanent girlfriend? As for Candy, Empress now believed the woman really did want this life.

"I just sent him a pin of our location," Julian said.

"Christ, he could be ages yet then." Pearl stamped her feet and slapped her palms together. "I just want my bed."

"Same," Candy said. "All that walking's made me tired."

Empress peered through the darkness at this motley crew she'd found herself with. "Why haven't either of you run?"

Candy let out a weird growl. "For fuck's sake, how many times do I have to say I like what I'm doing now? I don't want to bloody run, okay?"

Julian looked at Pearl. "What about you?"

"Because you have a gun and I know I'll be buried with the others, so what's the point? It's better to be alive in this life I've been brought to than dead, right?" Pearl pointed at Empress. "Why aren't you running?"

Empress shrugged. "For the same reasons as you. Besides, I like Julian and don't want to make him shoot me."

Chuckles went round at that.

"Headlights," Julian whispered.

The SUV swooped into the lay-by. Mocha must have risked it and collected it from Alding Close. The window went down, and his face appeared. "Fuck me sideways... Do you know what a hassle it was for me to pick this motor up with coppers crawling about all over the place? Get in."

Everyone bundled inside, Empress glad of the warmth coming from the heater. The screen behind the front seats lowered, and she knew they were in for a bollocking.

Mocha turned to look into the back. "Empress, thank you for letting Julian know you saw the blue lights. If you hadn't, well, you can imagine where you'd all be now, and the High Priest wouldn't be very happy that his main workers had been taken down the nick. As it is, he's steaming angry because he's worried Jerry and Fantasy might blab. So, we need to regroup again. There's talk of the rituals being held out the back of the house. The stones can be erected permanently then."

"But what about the traffic?" Empress asked. "Won't people see the light from the ring of torches, maybe even hear the music when it's summer and they have their windows down?"

"I've said this to the High Priest," Mocha said. "Hopefully he'll have another think and abandon that idea. I told him it isn't advisable to do anything at the house except live there."

"What about Fantasy?" Pearl asked.

"Yeah, tell me how that went down," Mocha said.

"She fucked off too fast for any of us to stop her," Candy said. "Julian said we had to go, there were police, and she darted for the front door. We had to leg *it out the back or get caught trying to bring her back inside."*

Mocha shifted to stare at Julian in the passenger seat. "Is that your take on it an' all?"

Julian nodded. "Better that we see who's loyal and who isn't. These three haven't given me any trouble since we left the house."

Mocha smiled. "A proper family, then. Right, let's get you back safe, then I need to switch the number plate to the original and hide the motor behind the barn for a bit. No outings for us for a while until the High Priest says otherwise. Blindfolds on."

He turned back to face the front, stuck his seat belt on, and drove off. Everyone else also belted up, covered their eyes, and Empress smiled to herself. They **were** *a family, albeit a dysfunctional one, but she did feel safe with this lot now, a part of things, like she belonged. It had been such a long time since she'd felt that—God, it was going to be difficult when the time came to call it a day. They'd all know she'd betrayed them behind the scenes, and for some reason, the idea of that stung.*

Shit, was she getting attached?

DI Taylor: What the hell happened? Where are you?

DI Taylor: Sorry, I get that you probably can't use your phone.

DI Taylor: Fantasy is safe.

DS Little: Only just been able to look at these—as you can imagine, Mocha is now tense. As to what happened, I felt duty-bound to go with the others to make sure they were okay. I still don't know where we're being kept, so until I do, I think it's best I stay put. Well, it's not like I can escape anyway, is it.

DI Taylor: I agree, but when I told you we were on the way, I expected you to reveal who you were and arrest Julian.

DS Little: But you didn't say that, sir. If you had, I'd have followed your instructions. As it was, I didn't know if you'd want me to blow my cover.

DI Taylor: Fair enough, but we're now back to square one. Fantasy has no idea where the house is either, so we're no further forward. Every SUV owner has been spoken to.

DS Little: If that were the case, then an officer would have been to this house and seen the shutters on the inside of the windows.

DI Taylor: The vehicle must be in someone else's name and address.

DS Little: The High Priest… So look into the owners again?

DI Taylor: On it. Stay safe.

Chapter Twenty-Four

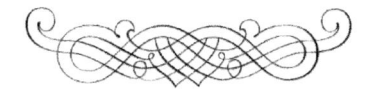

The recent conversation regarding Empress being a copper had shit her up. It was crystal clear that Pearl was trying to discredit her so she remained the only woman Mocha had eyes for. Maybe she was jealous because Mocha had told Empress earlier how well she'd fitted with the group. Pearl probably thought he was going to shift his sights to Empress, so the claws had come out.

I'm too tired to play games.

It had been a late night. She'd stayed up for hours chatting to Julian well after everyone else had gone to bed. Too wired to settle, she'd just wanted to talk and talk, maybe to stop her thoughts from straying to how stupid she'd been. She really should have followed protocol and got the women to safety. There was no denying it, she was probably going to get called into a disciplinary meeting regarding that, no matter that Taylor had seemed okay with her decision.

As the dark hours had passed, the more Julian had revealed about himself and his family life, the more she'd been strongly tempted to tell him his wife and kids were safe. She'd stopped herself at the last minute, still unsure whether she could trust him with that information—and having to explain how she knew it. But keeping the knowledge from him seemed wrong. He lived on tenterhooks, worried that any second his family would be obliterated if he put a foot wrong. She could ease that burden, she had that power, but until she felt one hundred percent okay with him, she'd keep it quiet.

There had been a meeting this morning where they'd discussed the news floating around on social media regarding the police in Alding Close. Mocha had a proper phone that had access to the internet (of course he fucking did), and he read out paragraphs relating to the police receiving a tip-off that illegal activities had been going on in Jerry's front room, women being forced against their will. Only someone on the inside would know that information, and it might not be long before the focus of an accusatory conversation swung her way. Pearl had already revealed she thought Empress was a copper, so it wouldn't be long before she put the seed into the soil that would grow into an unruly weed that Empress wouldn't be able to hack away in time. They might twig she had a phone and search for it.

She was going to have to go and delete all the messages.

And strongly suggest Fantasy had given away all the secrets.

DI Taylor had featured in one of the online interviews, although, thank God, he hadn't mentioned there being a police operation where one of his officers had infiltrated what was being called a sex trafficking gang. She should have known he wouldn't be stupid and break her cover, but she'd still held her breath when Mocha had read that particular article.

Being in this situation gave her insane thoughts, paranoid ones, and the feeling that at any moment, who she was would be discovered. She'd be killed and buried out the back. Another woman would then be snatched to take her place. But that would be a good thing. It would keep the story in the news. Sadly, too often the next big thing came along to eclipse certain stories (a celebrity affair trumped illegal sex), so Mocha would be less tetchy soon. He'd paced a lot today, waiting for word from the High Priest who'd been ominously silent.

For the past few hours, Empress had gone off to the dormitory bathroom and looked at her phone a lot more than usual, hoping for news from Taylor that the High Priest had been arrested, which was why Mocha hadn't heard from him, but the team still couldn't find the mastermind behind this outfit.

Empress had sent Taylor a message to get Jerry to safety in case the High Priest decided he needed to be dealt with—Alding Close being in the news, and the announcement about a sex ring and rituals, would mean he might get the blame for leaking the secret. Worryingly, he hadn't been at home when Taylor had gone round, and he hadn't answered his phone or his door on any occasion since. He appeared to have gone missing, and if the High Priest was involved in that, how come Mocha wasn't informed? Or was he, but he was keeping it to himself? Making out he'd been forced to do things here, when really, it was all bullshit?

Taylor had let her know what had gone on in Jerry's interview last night. Jerry hadn't given any details about the High Priest or anyone involved. He'd claimed not to have heard about any rituals. He'd refused to cooperate, saying he'd just paid for women to come to his house and that was the end of it. Empress suspected the High Priest had videos of *all* the disciples and none of them were going to get away with grassing him up unless they were prepared to face the repercussions—ruined lives, secrets spilled, all that sort of thing. Maybe Jerry had taken himself off somewhere until the heat died down.

Or had he been killed?

They were no further forward in finding out who the High Priest was because Mocha wasn't prepared to talk about the man's true identity. Did he even know it?

Empress had kept herself busy today. She'd cooked spaghetti bolognese in place of a Sunday roast, with homemade cheesy garlic bread on the side. A trifle sat in the fridge. Julian had relaxed his observations when she'd cooked and allowed her to use a knife to chop the onion without standing there hovering, and he hadn't taken it off her as soon as she'd finished. A stupid move on his part, Mocha's as well, because they'd just sat there and watched her using it, then did bugger all when she'd placed it on the worktop. Maybe, because she'd told Julian about the blue lights and had willingly gone with him last night, the pair of them thought she was in this with them for the long haul—or sufficiently scared enough of getting shot that she was going to do as she was told.

Empress glanced over towards the cooker. The knife still lay there. She diverted her attention to Pearl but looked at Mocha in her peripheral to check if he was watching her. She had a thought, then, that the knife had been left out on purpose to see which woman would take it, if any.

She was going to completely ignore it. Leave it for the others to deal with. Because she'd cooked the dinner, Candy and Pearl had said they would load the dishwasher and clean the kitchen. Julian got up and put the plates on the worktop, stacking them beside the sink ready to be rinsed after they'd had their pudding.

He didn't touch the knife.

Which was bloody dumb. Now she came to think about it, this wasn't exactly a well-run business. They didn't even know where she lived; they didn't know her real name; they couldn't look her up online and discover anything about her. She'd never revealed who she really was because they hadn't asked, which was odd. All they'd wanted to know was whether she had any family and friends who'd cause trouble. She'd told them she didn't, and they'd accepted that.

Was that because Mocha and Julian could then say to the High Priest that they'd asked the questions, received answers, and that was their part done? Was it just easier to be able to reassure him that the current women weren't anyone they needed to worry about?

"When did you last hear from the High Priest?" Pearl appeared completely at ease with how she'd just lit the fuse of a massive bomb, considering Mocha had made it quite clear he was pissed off there had been radio silence in that department.

"Too long ago." Mocha gave her one of those glances that told her to shut up.

"What if he's been picked up by the police?" Candy asked. "It would make sense then why he hasn't got hold of you. Fantasy could have heard a lot more than what we have—for all we know, she could have been listening to conversations at the rituals before they were stopped."

"Like what?" Empress asked, "where he lives and whatever?"

"Yeah. She could have told the police everything. She could have known where he lived all along but kept it to herself. If you remember, she was always trying to find ways to escape, so it's not surprising she was the first one to leave as soon as she could, and she'd be the first one to tell the police stuff, too. I bet she kept track of all the patterns that go on here."

Empress could have kissed her for opening up this line of conversation. "Like when food is delivered and whatnot?"

"Yes," Candy said.

Empress folded her arms. "Who even buys the shopping and arranges it for it to be dropped off here anyway?"

"The High Priest does," Mocha said.

"How do you get paid? Bank transfer?"

"No, cash."

"Do you even know who he really is?" Pearl got up to help him load the dishwasher.

"No."

Empress backed off. She wasn't getting anywhere with this conversation. "Let's have some pudding, shall we?"

Chapter Twenty-Five

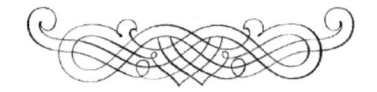

The Caridean Road stretched past Daffodil Woods and around a bend for a fair few miles before it ended at a T-junction. The shuttered house came into view on the left, a lot of trees dotting the property, the long driveway Laura had mentioned presenting as a grey ribbon in the murk. Dwayne had stolen a Transit and currently drove. They didn't usually get him involved in missions, not to this degree, but they needed his brawn and the appearance of him being a big fella, not to mention he'd been on duty and ready to steal the Transit, so it had saved them calling in anyone else. George and Greg sat in the back with Moody—George had promised him a bonus for disturbing him again today. They each wore balaclavas, army fatigues and boots, and gloves.

All of them had machine guns.

Dwayne turned into a lay-by and parked, the van concealed from the house's occupants by high bushes along the verge—not that anyone could see out with those shutters closed. Everyone exited the van. George handed Dwayne some large shears so he could clip out a section of bush.

They'd follow the plan they'd discussed earlier—unless Mocha or Julian also whipped out a weapon, not much could really go wrong. George had kept it plain and simple, but he was prepared to shoot the pair of them in the knees and ask questions later if he had to.

Dwayne finished making a narrow doorway in the hedge and passed the shears back. George tossed them into the van and braced himself for what was to come. He double-checked his machine gun had ammunition, even though he'd already done it before they'd left home. Weapons like this made him uneasy, but he wanted to use them as it wasn't the expected gun for The Brothers to choose. The same with the army clothes. This would give the illusion they were from some other kind of outfit, hired hitmen.

They moved through the gap in the hedge, George naffed off at a branch digging into his arse. They crouched and moved forward. Darting behind trees, then pausing to check the way was clear, they repeated the pattern and made their way across to the left-hand side of the house, the darkness concealing their shadow forms. Greg remained with Moody, keeping an eye on the front door, while George and Dwayne investigated the back area. As it was dark, George switched on his head torch—he doubted any light would be seen through the shutters, and to be honest, it wouldn't matter if it was. If someone came outside to investigate, they'd soon realise they were up against professionals.

He turned his head to get a good sweep of the grounds. Opposite stood a brick structure, the type that had likely housed a horse or two once upon a time. Was that where the three women were buried, behind it? Thankfully, because an undercover copper was here, she'd been able to pass on details of this place to the police so the bodies could be found and given a decent burial.

George nosed behind the barn—nothing there but scrubby grass and mud; he shook his head sadly at the thought of bodies being underground. He prayed that story had been a lie to make the current women behave and that the three ladies still in the news were being held somewhere until the heat died down.

He returned to Dwayne who stood by the back door. George raised his finger to indicate he wanted him to stay there keeping watch, something that had been discussed earlier, but still, when out in the field situations changed, and George didn't want to leave anything to chance.

He switched off his head torch and jogged to the front. He walked to the door, Greg and Moody behind him. A metal box for the post had been screwed into the wall—no letterbox in the door. Beneath the box, a wooden plaque proclaiming the house to be called The Hideaway—fucking apt. He checked Greg and

Moody were ready, and after receiving a thumbs-up, knocked on the door.

Going by Fantasy's story, George expected either Mocha or Julian to open up; the women were never allowed to do it apparently, and the chain would be kept on. He got his machine gun into position and pointed it towards where someone would stand to peer out at them. Hopefully there'd be a light on in the hallway which would splash out and show them in all their balaclava-faced glory, a nice tableau to shit the life out of them.

"Who is it?" came a voice from the other side.

"Amazon delivery."

"We've got nothing due. Put it on the ground and leave the premises."

"I need a signature. Over eighteens only."

The door opened a couple of inches, creamy light behind the silhouette of a male figure with short hair. He stood around five-ten. George wedged his foot in the gap so the bloke didn't have time to shut the door again.

"What the fuck?" the man said.

"I'm sure the High Priest would have told me to say hello had he still been alive, but unfortunately for him, he's been cut up into little pieces, and you'll be next if you don't open this fucking door and let us in."

"Shit. Who are you? Did he send you?"

"No, he didn't. My name is something I won't be revealing because you've got a copper in the henhouse and we don't want her knowing our identity. Oh, and before you even think about keeping me talking so the others can get out the back way, they can't because one of our men is there with another one of these beautiful guns. Also, you might want to think about your mother before making any rash decisions. Laura, isn't it? Lovely woman. She's given us the go-ahead to pick you up, not that we need her permission, but she feels if you've been up to no good then you should be held accountable for it. Told off and whatnot. Assuming you're Mocha, that is."

"Aww, please don't do anything to her…"

"Stop jumping the gun. She's fine. For now. Take the chain off like a good boy, eh?"

Surprisingly, he did, then stepped back to sit on the stairs. He raised his hands to either side of his head. George entered, giving the hallway the once-over and catching sight of another man standing in the doorway to what appeared to be a kitchen. He also lifted his hands, backing up until he stood beside a row of floor cabinets.

George advanced on him, leaving Moody to keep guard on Stair Boy while he entered the kitchen with Greg. They clocked where everyone was sitting: three women around a table, a big bowl in the middle with trifle in it, smaller bowls on placemats with half-eaten pudding in them.

"Seems we interrupted dinner." George moved to the back door and tapped out a prearranged sequence on it so Dwayne knew to still be on guard but that any major threat was neutralised for the moment.

"Who are you?" one of the women asked.

I bet that's the copper. "Who are *you*?"

"Empress."

No surprise there then.

She flicked her eyes towards the worktop. George followed the movement. A knife sat on the side. He picked it up in a gloved hand and put it in the dishwasher. If anyone went for it, they'd be stalled by having to open the door and pulling the tray out. On second thoughts, he put the pile of dirty plates and cutlery in a stack on the bottom shelf—those knives and forks could hurt.

He shut the door and faced Empress. "Go and get your phone."

She stared at him. He couldn't work out whether she was being defiant or sensible by not giving the game away. For a split-second it was obvious she was working out which response would be the better one—but was that for her or everyone else?

"I'm not fucking about here," George barked. "Go. And. Get. Your. Phone."

She stood and left the room, perhaps thinking he'd been sent by her colleagues, considering he knew she had a mobile. Greg went after her.

"What are your names?" George asked the other women.

"I'm Pearl, and I don't know what you think's going on here, but everyone in this house is innocent; we've all been forced to do things by the High Priest."

"God," the man butted in. "If this is one of his tests... You really don't want to be saying stuff like that, Pearl. It could get you killed."

George gave him a nod to acknowledge he appreciated what had just been said, that it was obvious he cared for the ladies, then he looked at the third woman.

"I'm Candy, and I actually love it here, so if you've come to scare the life out of us for the High Priest to see where our loyalties lie, then you can go back and tell him that I'll live here forever if that's what he wants."

Not a team player. Out for herself. Noted.

Everyone had been described to a T by Fantasy; these responses were what she'd told him to expect when he'd phoned her at the safe house earlier. Now for the bloke by the door who seemed to have crumpled in on himself, his hands still up, fear scored deep into his features. His face had a grey hue to it, and it appeared he was just about holding things together. If he'd been threatened in the past like Jerry and the others, then this situation might well be the last straw for him.

"What about you?" George asked. "What's your name?"

"J-Julian. Please, I..." He let out a sob, sounding anguished. "I can't fucking take any more. Just kill me and be done with it, all right? But please, leave my wife and kids alone and don't show her the video or photos. It's bad enough that she thinks I walked out on her without a word, or that I disappeared. She's been through enough because of me."

George kept Pearl and Candy in his peripheral, the gun pointed their way regardless that he wasn't going to use it on them, but he needed them to stay put. To Julian he said, "Your wife and sons are fine. They've been taken somewhere safe."

"You're messing about with me. You're fucking with my head."

"I'm not. The police have helped them."

Greg and Empress came back, cutting off anything else Julian might have said, and he cried softly with his eyes closed, his shoulders shuddering.

Greg held the copper's burner. "I've already asked her—somehow, phone locations can't get picked up from here. There's likely a jammer or something in place. I'm not prepared to turn it on yet, just in case there isn't."

George nodded. "Listen to me, you lot, and I want an honest answer." He stepped back a few paces to kick the door shut so Stair Boy wouldn't be able to hear what was being said. "That's Mocha out there, yes?"

Candy nodded.

"What's the score with him?" George asked. "And I don't want any bullshit lies because you're scared of him. It's important you tell me the truth because it'll affect what happens to him later on."

"He doesn't mean to be horrible," Empress said. "I've established since being here that both of these men have been forced into things by someone called the High Priest—if they don't behave, private information about them will be filtered back to their families or those families will be killed. It's unspecified at the present time as to whether these are just threats, but they've been effective. What I am trying to say is that even if the women have been treated unfairly—and indeed, three have been killed, so we've been told, so there *is* more than unfairness going on here—then it was done under duress. I don't condone murder, but having seen how things work around here, I'm not surprised that they've carried out orders despite how they feel about it. They're saving their loved ones, it's as simple as that, and sadly, if it means someone else has to die instead of them, then that's what's gone on."

"You *are* a fucking copper," Pearl said, seething.

Empress didn't respond. She'd gone from being 'one of the girls' back into copper mode.

"Whatever's gone on here, just rein in your tempers," George said. "We'll all be going outside in a minute. I'll leave the front door open."

"Why?" Empress asked.

"If you shut up for long enough, I'll explain." George gave her a filthy look, although she wouldn't get the full benefit of it because of the balaclava hiding his face. "All phones will be switched off. We'll walk to our van in the lay-by. The men will get in. You'll get your phone back, Empress, and after we've driven off, you can ring your boss then come back into the house to stay warm." He was going to tell a lie now, something to take suspicion off himself and his brother for coming to their rescue. He didn't want their names being associated with this—that would mean being questioned about where Feeny was, *and* that ponce, Gideon. "If you're wondering who we are, one of the red disciples sent us. The High Priest has scared him one time too many, and this is the result."

"We wondered whether Jerry would do that, didn't we," Candy said.

George made out he was oblivious. "Who the fuck's Jerry?"

No one was prepared to say.

"Why do we have to bother going all the way to the van only to come back?" Empress asked.

"Because you could ring the pigs as soon as we walk out of this door, and I want as much time between us driving away from here and the police turning up as possible. As you can imagine, men like us who're employed to go into these situations aren't exactly on the right side of the law, but even though we break it, we're still doing the right thing."

She nodded with what seemed like respect in her eyes. "Where are we?"

"The Hideaway, Caridean Road. Do you all understand what I've just said? I don't want anyone deviating from the plan because then I'll get shitty, and you've been through enough without me adding to it. I don't want to have to come and find you later down the line…"

Nods all round except for Candy.

"But what about *me*?" she said. "I *like* living here. I don't *want* to go home." She stuck her bottom lip out. "I probably haven't even got one anyway. I've got a room in a house, and it's likely been given to someone else because I haven't been able to pay the rent for yonks."

"I'll help you," Empress said. "We just need to concentrate on getting you out of here first."

"We?" Pearl queried. "So you've known that this rescue was going to happen all along and never told us? Why, in case I ratted you out to Mocha?"

Empress shook her head. "I had no idea. I don't know who these men are."

"You can speculate about that once we've gone," George said. "We need to get going."

"But where are you taking Mocha and Julian?" Empress asked.

George laughed. "Like I'm going to tell *you*."

Greg must have had enough and wanted to put an end to this because he took Julian's phone off him then opened the kitchen door and moved into the hallway. He asked Mocha for his mobile, switched both off, then placed them on a small table. He opened the front door and stepped outside. Moody jabbed the butt of his gun in the top of Mocha's arm to indicate that he wanted him to follow. George gestured with his for everyone else to troop out. The women went first, Empress taking charge by holding Pearl's and

Candy's hands, and then Julian tagged on to the back of the little crowd.

As promised, George left the front door open. He whistled to let Dwayne know they were finished. George traipsed behind everybody, Dwayne jogging to catch up and coming abreast of him. Moody and Greg put Julian and Mocha into the back of the van, getting in with them — they'd be blindfolded.

"At least do us a solid and wait until we've driven away," he said to Empress.

She nodded. "Thank you for finding us."

"You're welcome."

They planned to head off as if they were going somewhere other than Cardigan. The van would be dumped on the next housing estate and switched for another. Someone from the crew would be waiting there to take it off and get it crushed, likewise with the second one after they'd got into their taxi which had been left behind a row of shops on Cardigan. From there it was on to the warehouse.

Lots of questions lay in the future, but George suspected the one that played in Julian's and Mocha's minds the most was whether they'd ever see the light of day again.

Weirdly, George hoped so, despite three women being dead. Sometimes, even though people did fucking bad shit, they didn't deserve to die for it.

Chapter Twenty-Six

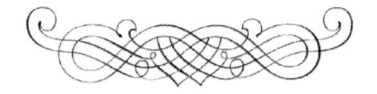

Much as George would like to reveal his face, he kept the balaclava on, plus the army outfit. Of *course* he wanted to let these two know who they were dealing with, it was a boost to his ego when people shit themselves once they realised who he was, but this wasn't the time or place for that. This situation called for secrecy, and if Julian and Mocha were let go, all they'd be able to tell anyone was that they'd been in a room with stone walls. Neither man had been strung up, but they each had a manacle on a wrist. Their feet were still on the closed trapdoor. They hadn't been stripped of their clothing, but that would change if it was clear they didn't want to cooperate.

Dwayne was off dealing with the disposal of the vehicles along with the other crew member, and Moody had gone home again. This part was best done by just George and Greg.

The light coming from the halogen heater cast an orange glow down the side of Mocha's body. He shivered despite the heat—probably fear—and he couldn't seem to look George or Greg in the eye. Guilt? Julian was another matter. He'd cried a lot behind his blindfold in the van but now seemed to have grown a backbone, maybe because the news that his wife and sons were safe had finally sunk in or he'd allowed himself to actually believe it. He was well able to look at George, his expression the type that showed how weary he was, but his eyes held a glimmer of hope.

"I'll start with you," George said to him. "Tell me your story."

What Julian told him was pretty standard in gangland terms—man does something he's not proud of, there's evidence of it which is later used against him. Except Feeny wasn't in gangland. Whatever, the method employed to get Julian to do what was needed came as no surprise to George because he'd have done exactly the same himself in order to get someone to do his bidding.

"Where are the women, the ones in the news?"

"He killed them." Julian jerked his free thumb at Mocha. "But he had no choice. The High Priest came over to the house, he had a mask on and a hood up, and he forced Mocha to shoot them out the back. The High Priest brought the gun with him, and it must have had some sort of silencer on it because it didn't make that much noise. Not enough to carry anyway. I helped dig the holes behind the barn, so I ought to go to prison for that as well as holding the women captive, because I did those things and they're wrong. Doesn't matter whether I was made to do it or not."

"The CPS might see it differently. They might not feel it's in the public's interest that you go to prison for it. That's the best-case scenario if we drop you off at the police station, but there *is* another avenue we can go down. You change your identity and fuck off."

"That means I'll never seen my wife and kids again. That's what you're saying, isn't it?"

George nodded.

"I'd rather go to the police and take my medicine."

"It's such a fucking shame it's come to this," George said, "because it's obvious you're a good bloke—you've got to be if you'd prefer to give yourself up."

"I've done so many bad things that I need to pay for them, otherwise I'd never be able to live with myself. Just walking away from it all feels wrong on so many levels, not to mention I'd be abandoning my children if I disappeared again."

"Makes a change to meet a decent man," Greg said. "In our line of business we've learned they're few and far between." He glared at Mocha. "What about you? What's your story?"

"Basically I had no choice either. There was no way I was going to let them kill my mum when she'd done nothing wrong." He sighed. "It's weird, but you get used to it in the end, being a bastard. You actually start to become that person, you think that's who you really are because you're so used to acting like a wanker. You forget who you were before."

George could understand that. There had been times he'd wondered who he would've been had he not gone down this path. If they'd managed to get Mum to move away from London years ago, into their dream cottage in the country, they'd be very different men today. And it was true, you became who your circumstances dictated you should be, a chameleon who adapted to the surroundings.

"Do you feel remorse?" George asked.

"Of course I do, especially when I think of Mum. She didn't bring me up to be like this. And it pisses me off, one little mistake caught on video, and it was used to force me to do shit."

"Moving on. Shooting the women—how do you feel about that?"

"Bloody awful. They didn't deserve it; just because they made it to the news, they were killed, but if the High Priest had done his homework in the first place and told me who to take after researching the women, then they wouldn't be dead. Instead, he got me to nick whoever was available, no research done whatsoever. Every time I shouted at them, threatened them, or told them to shut up, every time I was nasty, it was like a poison infected my blood or something. I know it sounds stupid, but that's how it felt, so the nastier I was, the more it became *who* I was."

"What's your preference?"

Mocha frowned. "What do you mean?"

"Are you going to fuck off out of London with a new name or go to the police?"

"It depends whether my mum can come with me. If she can, then I'll fuck off. I don't want to go to prison."

"Would your mum even want to give up her life here? She told us you had to pay for what you've done. Can you honestly see her letting you piss off into the sunset without being held accountable? Do you really think she'd go with you and pretend none of this ever happened?"

"If she heard the truth, then yes."

"Fair enough, you know her better than we do. We'll take you to the police station, Julian, or as close to it as I'm prepared to go."

"Where should I say I've been? What do you *want* me to say?"

"Tell the truth. You were put in a van, blindfolded, and taken to a room by men in army clothes with machine guns."

"What about me?" Mocha asked.

"We'll go to your mum's, see what she has to say."

George took blindfolds out of his pocket and walked behind the men to put them on. This was a weird one, letting criminals go, but at least one of them might be doing time, and the other would likely be doing it anyway even though he'd be classed as free. The conscience was a bastard and liked to remind you of your secrets. Mocha would be in a prison whichever way you looked at it.

With Mocha crouching between them so the neighbours didn't get an eyeful, George and Greg held one of his arms each and guided him up his mother's garden path. A tap on the door brought Laura to open it, and in her dressing gown, she stared down at her blindfolded son.

"Someone's come home to ask for a plate of food," George said, hoping she remembered their conversation from earlier.

She glanced at him and Greg in their balaclavas, her eyes going wide, and then quickly stepped back to let them in. George shut the door and left Greg to take Mocha into the kitchen.

"George?" Laura whispered.

"Yep, but don't use our names in front of him. He doesn't know who we are. It's a fucking long story, which we'll get him to tell you in a minute, but he thinks we've been sent by a red disciple."

"A what?"

George smiled. "As I said, it's a long fucking story."

Mocha had made his final decision. He was leaving London, but not until George and Greg had arranged new names for him and his mother. It was going to cost, but the twins were footing the bill for documents and a fake social media footprint to be planted online. The rest would be paid for by Laura—new place to rent, all that sort of thing. In the meantime, Mocha was going to stay in a safe house while his mother arranged their disappearance. Which reminded George that they needed to let Fantasy know that it was all over and she could go home.

"What made you change your mind about your son having to pay the price?" George asked Laura as they sat drinking tea in the living room. "You were pretty adamant when we spoke to you before."

"It's different when I know he didn't choose to do it. I don't think he should go to prison for twenty-five years or more for killing those poor women because, like he said, the High Priest basically stood there and made him pull the trigger. My brain keeps telling me that someone should pay for it, but shouldn't that be the priest?"

"He's already dead," George said. "He'll be looked into, his real life, his laptop. There's got to be a list of red disciples and watchers somewhere. It'll be sent to the police anonymously. Any laptops or devices that have certain videos on them will be destroyed."

"Thank you." Laura reached across the sofa to squeeze George's arm. "Thank you for saving my son."

George stood. "Come on," he said to Mocha. "We're off to the safe house."

While mother and son hugged, George and Greg waited by the front door.

"Did we do the right thing?" George asked.

"I think so."

"You *think* so?"

"Yeah. He's not going to be telling anyone what he's done. Despite the bravado, I saw the fear in his eyes. The thought of going to prison shits the life out of him."

George nodded and thought about the news three families were going to get—that their daughters' bodies had been found. Lives wrecked, all because of Feeny.

Bastard.

Chapter Twenty-Seven

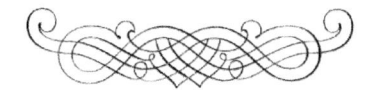

Detective Sergeant Vee Little. It was strange being her again. No more worrying that she'd be caught with a phone either down her knickers or hidden in the dormitory. No more worrying that she'd put her foot in it and blab that she was a copper.

The weight that had lifted from her shoulders the minute those balaclava men had walked into the kitchen was unreal. Yes, there had been the very stark fear that the High Priest had sent people to kill them all, and she'd been working out a way to escape before anyone could be murdered, but once it became clear that they'd been sent by a disciple, she'd racked her brains to try and work out how they'd discovered where the boarded-up house was when the police couldn't. Had there been a sex party held there and that was why the disciple knew the location? There was so much still unanswered, but at least they now knew who the High Priest was. The house had been rented by a young man called Kieron Feeny who also rented a flat on the Cardigan Estate. Vee had been given the job of speaking to the estate agent who'd dealt with the let, and she was on her way there now.

She parked beside a large building, the frontage all glass. She entered via the double doors, a long wooden reception desk directly in front which reminded her of a hotel. Two women worked behind it, and Vee approached the one who looked more amenable, a blonde with a nice smile.

She held out her identification. "Good afternoon. I'm Detective Sergeant Little, and I've got an appointment with Mr Orton."

"The letting agency? Yes, he's expecting you. He's on the first floor, and his office is the third one along the corridor. It's got the business name on the door so you won't miss it."

"Thanks."

Vee followed the directions and knocked on the door that had LUX LETTINGS etched into a gold plaque.

"Come in!"

She popped her head around the door and smiled at a man sitting behind a mahogany desk. Grey hair swept back with gel. Grey suit. Grey skin. "DS Little. I've got an appointment…"

He got up and shook her hand. "Take a seat. Would you like a coffee?" He pointed to a Tassimo machine.

"No, but thank you for the offer." She sat on chair opposite his desk but wasn't about to get too comfy as she didn't intend to stay long. She wanted to gather the information and then leave; she was meeting Fantasy for coffee in the French Café later on.

Mr Orton perched behind the desk and steepled his fingers. "How can I help you?"

"It's regarding a tenant. Kieron Feeny. He appears to have gone missing."

"Oh dear, that's not very good, is it. Let me just have a look on the system for you. I'm in charge of so many different tenants that I tend to forget who's who." He typed on his keyboard and studied his monitor. "Oh, yes, I remember him now. He gave two months' notice, paid the rent in advance and said he wouldn't be staying until the end of the agreement, which would have been May. He handed the keys in at the reception here, which was a bit naughty because they're not supposed to bugger off until I've been round to do a check. As it happened the place was spotless, he'd even had it painted throughout, so I didn't have to chase him for anything. I let the agency know, the one who holds the bond money, so that they could return it to him. I rented it out again straight away. Nice couple."

"Did he say where he was going?"

"We prefer them to so we can catch up with them if there are any problems later down the line, but he said he wasn't sure where he was going yet and would likely go and live with his mum for a bit."

That was a lie on Feeny's part, because Vee had already been to visit her with Taylor, and she'd allowed them to check her home without a warrant. It was obvious nobody lived in her spare room and even more obvious that she had no idea that her son had scarpered. When told about the scheme he'd been operating, she'd sat with a thump on her sofa and burst out crying, saying how ashamed she was, and those poor women dying and everything.

"Okay, thank you for your time." Vee got up and saw herself out. She made a quick stop at reception to see which of the women, if any, had been the one to take the flat keys from Feeny.

The blonde nodded. "It was me. He popped them on the desk here in an envelope with the name and address of the flat on the front and asked me to pass them on to Mr Orton."

"Do you have CCTV?"

"Unfortunately not," she said.

Vee left, disappointed, but that was sometimes par for the course in police work. Sometimes you got the answers and sometimes you didn't. They had to accept Feeny was in the wind. The curious thing was, none of his bank or credit cards had been used. The rent for both properties must have been paid in cash, as no direct debits had been set up in his bank other than for amenities. If he'd made himself disappear then he'd done a bloody good job of it and must have money stashed away somewhere that he could live off until he established himself elsewhere. But what if the red disciple who'd hired those men in army gear had got to Feeny first? What if he was dead?

Vee wouldn't complain about that, he deserved to die after what he'd done, but it would have been more satisfying if she could have arrested him and done her part in sending him to prison. But you couldn't always have it all, could you. She'd done her best, and it would have to be good enough.

She got in the car and drove to town, parking then walking to the French Café. She spotted Fantasy sitting at the back straight away. She'd bought Candy and Pearl with her, which was a bit of a surprise—well, Pearl being there was, because she'd given the impression she didn't want to continue their friendship any longer. She must have had a change of heart. She'd been interviewed like the others that night but had asked Vee and the team not to reveal her real name to anyone. Vee could understand why, after she'd looked into Miranda Stevens. The poor woman had been through the mill prior to her abduction.

Vee went to the counter and ordered a coffee and a slice of cake, taking them over to the table and parking her arse between Fantasy and Candy, opposite Pearl. "How have you been, ladies?"

"Not too bad," Pearl said. "Weird as it sounds, I miss Mocha."

Vee hadn't been in on any of their interviews after the rescue, so she'd only read the reports afterwards, and she doubted very much they'd have the whole truth in them. "Before I say what I'm going to ask, this goes no further, I won't be running back to tell the team. But how far did things go between you two? I know you had sex and whatever, but what about emotionally?"

Pearl shrugged. "I think he was trying to tell me stuff without actually saying it. Like I knew he didn't want to be horrible to us, that it wasn't who he really was, but he didn't outright tell me that. I can't explain it, I think he just got used to being nasty and rolled with it."

"Shame we can't find him to ask him ourselves," Candy said. "Those balaclava men must have done something to him."

"I think that's the case," Vee said, "although this didn't come from me, if you catch my drift. When Julian turned up at the station a couple of hours after we were set free, when he was questioned, it came out that they'd been blindfolded and taken to a room with stone walls. They were asked to tell their side of the story and what they wanted to happen next. Julian chose to go to the police and admit his part in it, but Mocha asked to be set free. Because the police don't know who he actually is, with no name to go on we can't round him up and arrest him. Now, he'd be stupid to still hang around London because you three have seen his face, and so has Tara, so have I, so he isn't going to want to risk any of us spotting him. We think he's gone to ground elsewhere."

"I'm glad," Pearl said, "because there's no way he'd have walked free like Julian has. Mocha killed those women, Julian didn't."

The CPS had decided against prosecuting Julian. There was enough witness proof that he'd been coerced, and some information had come in anonymously, names of red disciples and watchers, and files describing how the High Priest was going to manipulate Julian and Mocha into working for him. Julian, his wife, and their sons had relocated, all of them changing their names. A fresh start.

Jerry was still missing, but a taxi driver had come forward to say he'd been contacted by a private detective who'd wanted to know where he'd taken Jerry on Valentine's Day last year. The location was a field in the middle of nowhere, and as such a long time has passed, Taylor had made the decision not to try and find any DNA there.

Vee had something new to share, which would be hitting the news around about now as Taylor was doing a press conference. She felt it was better that her friends heard it from her. "Look, there's something I've got to tell you. It's about the women who came before all of us."

"Oh God..." Fantasy laid hand on her chest.

"More bodies have been found. Not behind the barn but by one of the trees. There were four of them, so we can only assume that they were the first four. We're having to piece things together, trying to make a story that fits with all the evidence, but for all we know there could be even more bodies somewhere away from the property and *they're* the first ones."

"Jesus Christ, we got lucky," Candy said. "And there was me, glad to be living there. I have no idea what I was thinking."

"That's because you're happy in your new flat now," Fantasy said.

"Yeah, and I've got you to thank for getting me that."

Fantasy smiled. "I just so happened to know the landlords and was cheeky enough to ask if they had any places going cheap."

"Those women, though," Pearl said, popping the happy bubble. "I wonder what they were killed for."

"It doesn't bear thinking about," Vee said. "You're better off not tormenting yourself. Try to move on. I know it's going to be bloody hard, but you all deserve good things in life." Vee looked at Pearl especially to get that point across.

The little meeting continued, each one of them talking about what they'd done since they'd given their lengthy statements on the night the balaclava men had knocked on the door. Vee had realised she'd finally got over the lack of Ross in her life—she'd been so busy she hadn't had time to think about him. She returned home from work exhausted by the team's efforts to discover where any other missing women were, but eventually the dead ends would be too frequent, and while the case wouldn't be closed, they'd focus on something else instead.

An hour later, she said her goodbyes and left the café, taking in a deep breath of fresh air. It sounded daft, but it seemed to cleanse her, give her a new lease of life, and for the first time in what felt like forever, she didn't feel like a spare part anymore. She had friends now, people she wouldn't mind going out with for drinks. People she wouldn't fob off by saying she was too busy or too tired when in reality she'd been too depressed.

She even dared to hope that one day soon she'd actually be happy.

Chapter Twenty-Eight

Easter had come and gone, and Pearl had finally got over missing Mocha. You had to grow up and move on, didn't you, and there was no sense in pining for someone she'd never see again. She'd gone back to work on the Proust Estate, being an adult and telling the leader that she needed a permit. What she hadn't expected was to be asked if she wanted a job working for the leader.

Jet Proust was a bit of a weird one. She dressed in designer gear and looked like she was about to either get her hair or nails done or engage in some serious retail therapy. But looks could be deceiving. Pearl had seen her with a knife, slashing someone's cheek, smiling while she did it, then she'd casually wiped the blood on the man's jacket and put her blade back in her gem-encrusted handbag. Jet liked bling, makeup, fashion magazines, and fine dining. She came across as a high-maintenance woman, but she was far from that.

Tonight she wanted Pearl to go with her to an art exhibition where she'd be meeting with a new drug supplier, one she'd been in talks with on the phone for some time. This sort of thing was nothing unusual, Pearl had done it numerous times before, but something about it left a nasty taste in her mouth today. She'd learned, while kept in the boarded-up house, that if her gut said something was wrong or something awful was about to happen, then she should believe it. But how was she going to tell the boss that? Jet would laugh in her face and tell her to do as she was told.

There was no getting out of this.

Pearl took a deep breath and went to her wardrobe, which was actually the box room in her house that she had turned into a dressing room. She had so many clothes now, Jet had given her a lot, and she earned enough to buy her own whenever she wanted. She picked out a black dress and high heels, plus a bolero jacket in red. She hung them on the door to her bedroom and went to have a soak in the bath.

The calm before the storm.

To be continued in *Roost*,
The Cardigan Estate 40